GALLOWS STONE

Echoes of the Executed

AF439264

Phillip G. Andrade

AUXANO

GALLOWS STONE - *Echoes of the Executed*

For the ones in the back seats

who came once and were never asked their name.

They profess that they know God;

but in works they deny him.

— Titus 1:16

TABLE OF CONTENTS

GALLOWS STONE

Part One

The Stone

Chapter 1

Gallows Hill

Frank Silvia had spent thirty years studying men who never realized they were the villains in their own stories. On a Saturday morning in October, he drove north to add another name to that list.

The Sagamore Bridge appeared ahead, its tall grey arch marking his exit from the Cape. Past it, the scenery changed from water to scrub pine and the long, grey stretch of Route 3. Frank moved into the left lane and adjusted the rearview mirror, even though there was nothing behind him. He simply liked things to be in order.

His coffee had gone cold near Cedarville. He passed a sign for Plimoth Patuxet, the old Plimoth Plantation, but kept going. He'd driven by many times and never stopped, preferring to learn history from books instead of from people in costumes. On the passenger seat, a yellow legal pad held two pages of sermon notes in his tight handwriting: dates, names, and an outline for the first week of a four-part series on the American church and its blind spots. He was driving two hours to visit the site of the Salem witch trials. Frank believed that being in a place mattered. He thought you couldn't preach honestly about somewhere you'd only read about.

He drove past the cranberry bogs south of Kingston, their water black and still beneath the October clouds. The radio was off. Frank liked to think in silence, and he was wondering how someone as brilliant as Cotton Mather could still approve of hanging his neighbors. There was a sermon in that. There always was. Frank had a way of making history interesting for a congregation that might rather be watching football. He could bring an old theological debate into a room full of Cape Codders eating coffee cake, and they would listen. They might not change, but they would pay attention.

He drove a ten-year-old Camry he'd bought used in Hyannis. It was clean but a bit worn. A Gordon College parking sticker from his time as a visiting lecturer was still stuck to the rear bumper, since taking it off would have needed a razor blade and more effort than Frank wanted to spend. In the backseat, a canvas tote held library books: two about the Salem trials, one on Puritan church structure. The last was a book on New England meetinghouse architecture he'd checked out on a whim and would probably renew twice before returning unread.

Route 3 turned into Route 128, and traffic got heavier. Frank moved into the slower lane and stayed there. He wasn't in a hurry and knew it. He practiced his opening line out loud: In 1692, the most theologically educated community in North America executed twenty of its own citizens. When he saw the first Salem exit sign, he felt a quiet satisfaction that only research gave him. For him, it was always about the material, not the destination.

• • •

He parked near the Peabody Essex Museum and started walking. Frank passed a shop selling witch spell kits and a restaurant called Hex with a cocktail menu in the window. A family of four walked by in matching black capes. A teenager in a pointy hat took a selfie in front of a store selling crystals, tarot decks, and, oddly, saltwater taffy.

Frank wasn't offended by this. He just thought it was shallow. Twenty people had died here—fourteen women, five men, and Giles Corey, who was pressed under stones for two days because he refused to plead. That could be seen as either stubbornness or courage, depending on how you viewed silence. Frank could list their names in order of execution: Bridget Bishop first, on June 10, then Rebecca Nurse, Sarah Good, Susannah Martin, Elizabeth Howe, and Sarah Wildes—five on one day in July. He remembered these names easily after years in the archives. But he didn't feel any special grief for them. To him, they were data points in a historical argument, and it was the argument that interested him.

The Witch Trials Memorial on Charter Street was quieter than the tourist area. Stone benches were built into a low wall, each with a name, a date, and a method of execution. Frank walked around slowly, reading each one. He didn't pray. He read them like someone reading a well-designed exhibit, noticing the memorial's craftsmanship and what it included or left out. The air was damp and in the low forties, a New England cold that seeped in instead of stinging. The maples along the street were just starting to turn. He paused at Rebecca Nurse's bench. Nurse was seventy-one, a longtime church member, and the jury had first found her not guilty. The judges sent them back, and the second verdict was guilty. Frank had read her examination transcript three times—the confusion of a deaf old woman asked to explain things she couldn't see, in a courtroom with rules that would have embarrassed even a medieval inquisitor. The ministers didn't object; they just took notes. Frank found this interesting, as he did with most institutional failures—as a case study or warning. For him, it was a problem to analyze from the safe distance of three centuries.

• • •

It took twelve minutes to walk to Proctor's Ledge. Frank had read about the debate over the execution site: Gallows Hill, the traditional spot, versus the rocky outcrop behind today's Walgreens on Pope Street. He agreed with the University of Virginia researchers who used witness accounts to pinpoint the location. The executions had to be visible from the town center. Gallows Hill didn't have the right sight lines, but Proctor's Ledge did. Frank liked that this argument relied on geometry instead of tradition.

The site was simple: a small memorial wall at the bottom of a wooded slope, behind a pharmacy parking lot. The names were carved into granite again. There were a few offerings: flowers, coins, and a handwritten note in a plastic sleeve that Frank didn't read. Beyond the memorial, the ground rose into oak and scrub pine, just another ordinary New England hillside. That was the thing about historical tragedy. It almost never looked special.

Frank stood at the base of the ledge and looked back toward town. He could see the rooflines, the First Church steeple, and the harbor beyond. This view convinced him. The condemned would have been visible from the town center, with the crowd watching below and ministers in black coats among them. The cart would have come up a path where the pharmacy's access road is now, and the condemned would have walked the last part. Some prayed aloud. George Burroughs, a former minister, recited the Lord's Prayer from the ladder. According to the beliefs of the time, this should have been impossible for a witch. Cotton Mather, on horseback, told the crowd not to be disturbed by it. The execution went on. Frank always focused on that detail: Mather on his horse, speaking over a dying man's prayer. He did this not out of cruelty, but out of certainty.

He climbed the slope a little, stepping over roots and fallen leaves. He thought about Nicholas Noyes, the minister from the First Church in Salem, who had stood at the executions and reportedly called the victims eight firebrands of hell. Noyes wasn't ignorant. He had studied at Harvard and could argue theology with great skill. He simply believed, with all his education and authority, that those being hanged deserved it. That was the real horror of Salem: not superstition, but certainty. Educated, confident, and theologically precise certainty, used to justify killing neighbors while quoting Scripture.

Frank crouched down. He noticed something at the base of a granite outcrop, partly buried in leaves and reddish soil—a stone, round and about the size of his palm. He pulled it out with his fingers. It was dark, almost black, as if scorched, with a faint vein of quartz running through it like a healed crack. He turned it over. It was just a rock, nothing special. But it felt warm, not hot, just warm, like a stone left in the sun, even though the sun hadn't been out all morning and wouldn't be.

Frank stood up, brushed dirt from his knees, and slipped the stone into his jacket pocket without thinking. He had always picked up things at historical sites—arrowheads as a kid, pottery fragments in Israel during a seminary trip. He liked collecting small objects that connected to big events, keeping them in a desk drawer with sermon flash drives and a broken stapler he meant to replace. The stone joined that group. It was just something to fidget with while writing. He was already heading back down the slope, thinking about a sentence on Noyes, before he even noticed the weight in his pocket.

• • •

The path back to his car passed the lower edge of the memorial grounds, where a park bench sat under an oak tree that had lost most of its leaves. A woman sat on the bench. She looked about forty-five, wore a grey fleece pullover, and was crying.

It wasn't quiet crying. It was the helpless kind that comes when the news is still fresh and the body doesn't know how to react. She held a phone in one hand, pressed flat against her thigh, the screen still on. Her other hand covered her mouth. She stared at nothing.

Frank noticed her and slowed down, but didn't stop. He observed her automatically and in detail: the phone face down on her thigh, her shoulders pulled in as if she wanted to disappear, and no one else nearby. He felt a real, though weak, urge to stop, sit down, and ask if she was okay. After all, he was a pastor. He'd attended countless pastoral care seminars. He knew what he was supposed to do.

He kept walking.

He found reasons not to stop before he'd taken three steps. It was a two-hour drive back to the Cape. He didn't know her. She probably had someone she could call. Approaching a stranger crying alone in a park could be awkward. What if she didn't want help? What if he made things worse? What if she thought he was acting strange? What if she came here for privacy and he ruined it?

Every reason made sense. Each one fit neatly with the last. He was good at building justifications like this. He'd done it for years, in his office, at hospital bedsides, and in church parking lots after Sunday services when someone he should have noticed slipped away. His reasoning always followed the same pattern, and only later did he realize that this pattern was the real problem.

He kept walking.

He briefly thought someone else would stop. Salem was a small city. The woman was probably local. The bench was close to the pharmacy parking lot, and soon another customer would come out with a prescription. The world had its own ways of helping people. Frank told himself this, though he didn't say it out loud, because saying it would have forced him to admit he was making excuses.

He was thinking about Nicholas Noyes again before he reached the sidewalk. The irony was clear. A pastor, writing a sermon about how institutions fail to show compassion, walks away from a woman who needs help. He missed the lesson, even though it was right in front of him.

He didn't let himself think about it, but deep down he knew. He had spent an hour at a memorial for twenty people who died because their pastors chose to be theologians instead of neighbors. He had walked the hillside, read the names, and picked up a souvenir stone. Then, when a woman cried on a bench just ten feet away, he walked past her. The man who could write a four-week sermon on institutional moral failure couldn't see his own small failure as it happened.

By the time he reached his car, the woman was already in the past by three minutes, and the sermon by four. He turned the key and the Camry started. He had a long drive ahead. The suburban sprawl thinned as the highway angled southeast toward the Cape. Frank felt the particular satisfaction of a productive trip, the kind of day that justified itself and would produce something. He was already planning the sermon's introduction and believed it was well-crafted. He would start with the Walgreens: the absurdity of a pharmacy built over an execution ground, layers of Americans forgetting the past, and then move to the theological question. How did the most biblically literate community in the New World get it so catastrophically wrong? The congregation would hang on every syllable. He was sure of it.

Traffic eased after Braintree and the highway opened up. Frank moved into the right lane, feeling content as he thought through the sermon series. Week one: Salem, the sin of certainty. Week two: the First Great Awakening, the fire that faded. Week three: the prosperity gospel, the God who wants you rich. Week four was undecided, but it would be about the present. He'd figure it out. The main idea was how American Christianity kept creating institutions that talked about God but ignored the people they were supposed to care for. It was a good thesis: clear, solid, and the kind you could build four strong sermons around. It would leave the congregation feeling like they'd learned something, which was both Frank's highest and, if he was honest, his lowest goal for a Sunday.

• • •

His phone buzzed in the cupholder. He answered on the car's Bluetooth. It was Janet.

"How was Salem?"

"Good. Great, actually. Got some excellent material for the series."

"Did you eat anything?"

"I had a sandwich on the way up."

"We need milk. And there's a message from Linda about the piano tuning."

"I'll call her tomorrow."

Janet paused. These days, she often left quiet spaces in their conversations, where she used to ask something. Frank didn't wonder about her thoughts anymore. The pause was always there now, and he just let it be.

"Frank. Are you coming straight home, or stopping somewhere?"

"I might pull off in Mashpee for a beer. Forty minutes."

"Okay."

That was it. Their conversation was quick, the kind of shorthand that comes from years together. Janet asked about the weather. Frank said it was gray. She said the dog got into the trash. He said he'd take care of it when he got home. They hung up without fuss, nothing urgent left, knowing they'd see each other soon.

Frank saw the Sagamore Bridge ahead and crossed it. The light changed, just like it always did when you reached the Cape. Even on cloudy days, the sky seemed to open up, almost like the place had its own weather. Frank felt that familiar feeling of coming home. He smelled salt through the open window. The road narrowed, and the land flattened into scrub oak, pitch pine, and long sandy stretches that told him he was home.

He turned toward Mashpee. Naukabout was on Lake Avenue, with a patio over the water and a good IPA. Frank had a beer outside while the sun tried to break through the clouds but couldn't. He stayed about forty minutes, just him and a couple in Bruins hats at the other end. Then he went to Stop & Shop in Falmouth for milk and anything else Janet needed.

His legal pad with sermon notes was on the passenger seat. In his jacket pocket, the stone was already forgotten. He'd notice it again that night when he hung up his jacket and heard it hit the closet wall. He would put it on his desk in the morning. While working, he might pick it up and spin it between his fingers, like a paperweight. It would join the other small things from his tidy, well-read, carefully built life, and the stone would wait.

Frank drove toward Falmouth, scrub pine lining both sides of the road. He thought about Sunday.

GALLOWS STONE

Chapter 2

Cape Cod

Frank's house was on a quarter-acre lot off Sippewissett Road, about half a mile from the church. He and Janet bought the 1972 ranch in 1998 and spent twenty years fixing it up as their kids grew up and moved out. When Frank came in, the house felt warm. Janet sat at the kitchen island with her reading glasses on, the Saturday Cape Cod Times open in front of her, and a glass of red wine next to the obituaries. She always started with the obituaries. She was sixty and still beautiful, though Frank hadn't told her that in years. Saying it had become one of those habits that quietly fade over time in a long marriage.

"Long drive."

"It was fine. Got what I needed."

He set the milk on the counter and hung his jacket on the hook by the back door. The stone made a faint sound when it hit the wall.

Janet made a chicken and rice casserole. She didn't ask about Salem, and he didn't bring it up. They ate together at the kitchen island, both reading—Janet with the obituaries, Frank with a book. For almost ten years, since their daughter Annie moved out and the dining-room table became a place to pile things, they'd eaten side by side at the island three or four nights a week. They both said they liked it better, but neither explained why.

After dinner, Janet went to read in the den. Frank loaded the dishwasher, poured her a second glass of wine without asking, and brought it to her. She thanked him. He went into his study off the front hall, sat at his desk for an hour, reviewing his manuscript for tomorrow.

Around ten, he came into the bedroom. Janet was already in bed, reading on her side. Frank sat on the edge of his side and untied his shoes.

"What was she like?" Frank asked.

Janet set the book down. "Who?"

"The woman. Linda's piano tuner. You said Linda called."

"That was about the piano tuner. The one she always uses. She wanted *you* to call him."

"Right. Right."

He sat on the edge of the bed in his socks for a moment. Janet picked her book up again.

He thought about telling her about the woman crying in the park. He considered saying he had walked past her, or admitting he did that more often than he wanted. The words came to him and stayed there, unspoken, like most things he thought about in their marriage now.

He stood up and went to brush his teeth.

When he came back, Janet had already turned off her light. He turned off his. They lay on their backs in the dark for the usual two minutes. He kissed her on the temple, she squeezed his hand, and they rolled away from each other. That was the end of the day.

Frank slept well. There was a great sermon on the horizon.

• • •

The office at Cape Community Church was cold in the morning. Frank turned up the thermostat and listened as the old baseboards made their usual October noises, clicking and ticking through the building until the sanctuary would be warm enough to preach in. He set his coffee down and hung his jacket on the back of the chair. The stone made a dull sound against the wood and rolled into the seat. He picked it up and set it on the blotter next to the broken stapler, which he had been meaning to replace for a year..

The office faced south. Through the window he could see the parking lot and, past it, the long flat grey of Vineyard Sound under low clouds. Three cars already. arrived for the service. Grace Baker's white Buick was always first, because Grace was always first, and she had been first for something like forty years. Ray's truck was in its usual spot. There was also Megan's old moped leaning against the front handrail.

He turned the stone over once and set it back down. It felt warm under his fingers. He didn't think about it again.

The books on the walls were sorted by tradition, not by author. Patristics were on the south wall, where the light was best. Frank liked to think the Fathers would have approved. Reformation books were to the left of his desk. American church history was behind him, and that's what he was using this morning: Miller's New England Mind, Hambrick-Stowe on Puritan devotion, and a slim paperback of Mather's primary sources, underlined almost to the point of being unreadable. On his desk blotter were twelve pages of sermon manuscript, double-spaced in twelve-point Times. Frank didn't preach from notes. He used a manuscript, reading it like someone presenting a paper at a conference. He had tried preaching without one once in seminary, but a professor told him his off-the-cuff style sounded like a tax attorney reading a deposition. Frank took that as both a compliment and a warning.

He sat at the desk and ran through his opening: the Walgreens, the layered absurdity, the turn into the courtroom. It was good. Really good, he thought. Frank drank his coffee. Outside, another car pulled into the lot.

• • •

The church sat on a low rise above Route 28A, a white clapboard box with a modest steeple, built in 1924 by a congregation that had since scattered into three other denominations and, eventually, regathered here under a fourth. The bell in the steeple had not rung since 2011, when the rope had snapped and nobody had found the time or the motivation to restring it. The front steps had a black-iron handrail Ray Pacheco had installed himself after Grace slipped on the ice three winters back. The parking lot was crushed shell, because paving it would have cost what a new boiler would cost, and the boiler was always going to come first.

Inside, the sanctuary seated sixty on a good Sunday and had not been close to full since the revival in '97, which Frank had not been there for but heard about often. Pine pews stained dark with decades of lemon oil. A center aisle. A modest platform. No stained glass. The windows were plain, looking out on the parking lot to the east and a stand of pitch pine to the west. The piano was stage right, an upright Yamaha that Linda had paid to have tuned last Tuesday after Frank forgot to return her call. The sound booth was a carpeted closet in the back that had been meant to hold hymnals and now held a mixing board, two rack-mounted processors, and seventeen year old Megan Eldridge.

Past the foyer, a hallway ran thirty-two feet to the fellowship hall, which also served as the potluck space, the children's classroom, and once a month, the stage for a men's breakfast that drew six men and had for as long as anyone could remember. Frank had reviewed the building plans himself last winter when the roofers needed them. He could sketch the footprint from memory. It was a small building, and that was part of what he liked about it.

On a clear morning you could see the Vineyard from the front steps. Today it was not clear. There was nothing but a solid expanse of grey on the horizon.

•••

Grace Baker came in at quarter past nine, just as she always did, and squeezed both of Frank's hands. Her grip felt thin and familiar, like old parchment. She had been shaking hands in that foyer since Jimmy Carter was president. She wore a navy cardigan over a flowered dress and carried a leather Bible with so many tabs sticking out it looked like an old Rolodex.

"Good morning, Pastor. I was thinking about last week's sermon all day Tuesday."

"Well, I hope some of it stuck."

"Oh, it did. The part about the covenant. You know I always love theology."

Frank did know. Grace told him so most weeks. He thanked her and let her drift past him toward the sanctuary, where she took her seat in the second pew on the right, the same seat she had taken since 1982.

Ray came in behind her with a manila envelope under one arm and a Dunkin' coffee in the other. He was sixty-one and broad-shouldered. Most people called him Red, even though his once-bright red hair had faded to grey over the years. The nickname stuck. Nobody called him Ray anymore except Grace, who did it on principle.

"Furnace is ticking funny again," Red said. "I want to get Jim Souza out here before we need him."

"Whatever you think." Frank responded.

"I'll call tomorrow." He lifted the envelope. "I'll be in the office. Back before the call to worship."

He went down the hall to count last week's offering, which was his ritual and his authority, and Frank let him.

Linda was at the piano. She never spent time in the foyer. She always came in through the back door at nine, went straight to the bench, and played through two or three arrangements before the service started. Her eyes were closed, shoulders moving with the music. Linda played the keyboard with a sincerity Frank respected but never quite understood. He had known her husband Mike for a decade and was pretty sure the last time he and Mike had been together was at a wedding. She wore sunglasses pushed up on her head, even inside, which Frank figured was her way of showing some style. He didn't look at her eyes. If he had, he would have noticed they were red. Tom, the youth pastor at Cape Community, walked in earlier than usual. He was thirty-eight, holding a coffee in one hand and his phone in the other, dressed in the navy hoodie with the church logo he had designed. He'd ordered two hundred of them, and they were still handing them out three years later.

"Hey hey hey. Pastor Frank. Did you see the thing about the Pats last night?" Tom asked as he walked quickly toward the sanctuary.

"I did not."

"Oh, man. You don't even want to know." He waved across the sanctuary at Megan, who waved back from the booth without looking up. Tom drifted toward the back row and did not sit so much as arrange himself across two seats.

Megan was already running the morning. She had arrived at some point before Frank, which was normal because Megan went to church whenever there wasn't snow, and Frank had stopped noticing how much effort she put in a long time ago. She had the board levels set, the wireless mics charged, and the call-to-worship slide queued. She wore her headphones around her neck.

Megan came to church alone. She had been doing this since she was fourteen. Her parents were divorced, and Frank learned from a brief talk with Megan's mother three winters ago at Stop & Shop in Falmouth that neither parent was religious and neither had ever attended a service at Cape Community. Megan rode her moped from her mother's house in East Falmouth on Sundays, on Wednesday nights for choir tech, and on Tuesday afternoons whenever she thought the sound system needed work, which was often. Frank had known all this for three years but had never asked Megan about any of it. The church saw Megan as a capable worker at the booth and, without asking, assumed her skills were all she needed. For three years, Megan watched. Frank hadn't noticed yet. But Megan watched because she needed to feel in control. She needed to feel safe.

When he caught her eye across the room, she gave him a small nod that communicated that she was ready, and he nodded back.

Behind Megan, the Cabrals took their usual spot in the third row on the left. Joanne Medeiros came in with her two kids and gave her usual apologetic half-wave. The man Frank had been greeting for two years, whose name he still wasn't sure was Dave or Dan, came in, said, 'Morning, Pastor,' and shook Frank's hand. Frank replied with 'Morning.'

The service moved along its planned course. Opening hymn, a congregation favorite Linda could have played in a power outage. Tom ran the projector slides half a beat behind the verses, which he had been doing for two years and would do for two more. Grace sang with her eyes closed. Ray mouthed the words. Megan watched the mic levels. Frank offered the pastoral prayer from an index card he had written that morning, and it was competent and warm and ended nowhere in particular.

Then the sermon.

He stepped to the pulpit with his manuscript in a black leather folder and set it down flat. He looked up. He let the silence do the work it was supposed to do.

"In October of 1692," he said, "a man named Nicholas Noyes stood under the bodies of five women and three men who had just been hanged at the edge of what is now Salem, Massachusetts. He looked up at them, and he said, What a sad thing it is to see eight firebrands of hell hanging there."

He paused.

"Today, that spot is behind a Walgreens."

The congregation laughed, feeling the relief of people who had braced for a tough sermon but were instead allowed to smile. Frank noticed and used the moment. He led them up Pope Street to the ledge, pointed out the view of the town center, and shared the scholarly debate about why the location mattered. He brought them into the courtroom and explained spectral evidence as a trial lawyer would to a jury, showing it as a procedure that made sense to those in charge. He spoke about Mather, not as a caricature but as the real person. He quoted from Wonders of the Invisible World, letting Mather's own words speak for themselves. He described Rebecca Nurse's examination, the first acquittal, the judges sending the jury back, and the second verdict. He discussed the Hebrew word mekhashepha and the debate over whether it meant witch or poisoner, and whether the court's entire argument rested on a translation issue that even a first-year seminarian could have spotted. He took his time. He trusted the audience, and they leaned in, eager to listen.

"These were not ignorant men," he said. "That's the uncomfortable part. They had read more Scripture than most of us will read in our lives. They had prayed more than most of us. Cotton Mather could have taught New

Testament Greek at nineteen. And they hanged their neighbors. Not because they were evil. Because they were certain."

He paused again. He had written a note in the margin to remind himself to pause, but he kept his eyes up.

"That is what certainty looks like when it is untethered from mercy. That is what theology looks like when it forgets who it is for. That is the sin of Salem. Not superstition. Certainty."

He finished his point and let the words linger in the room. Then he prayed and took his seat.

Linda played the response hymn. The congregation stood, sang, then gathered their coats and slowly made their way to the back. Sitting behind the pulpit, Frank felt the familiar warmth in his chest that always came after a sermon that connected. He called it the Spirit, but he knew it was also adrenaline, and after so many years, he didn't try to tell the difference.

* * *

In the parking lot, people did what they always did. They stood by their cars and talked about the weather, which was about to change, and the Patriots, who were not. Pete Crowell was building a four-bedroom where the Carneys' old house had been. The Carneys hadn't been seen in two summers, and there was a long talk about whether the Bourne rotary would ever get finished. That project had lasted through three selectmen. No one mentioned the sermon. It wasn't because they didn't like it. They liked it a lot. It was delivered well and didn't leave anything unsettled.

Two parishioners told him it was one of his best. A retired English teacher said she had never known that about spectral evidence. Tom, halfway into his own car, leaned out and shouted, "You should do a podcast, Pastor. I'm not joking." Frank said he was not going to do a podcast. Ray reminded him about the furnace. Grace, who had come up behind him while he was talking to the English teacher, put her hand on his arm and did not let go for a moment longer than usual.

"That was important, what you said. About those ministers."

"Thank you, Grace."

"You said it kindly. You didn't make them into monsters."

"I appreciate that."

She held his gaze for a moment longer. Then she squeezed his arm and walked to her Buick. Frank folded the morning's bulletin into his jacket pocket and went to his car.

He was the last one out. Ray had left at eleven, Megan not long after, and by the time Frank walked back into the office, the sanctuary had settled into its Sunday-afternoon quiet, the baseboards ticking again, cooling this time instead of warming.

The stone was where he had left it, next to the stapler.

He picked up the stone and turned it over. It was still warm. The warmth could have come from anywhere. Maybe it was a stone left on a sunny desk, though there hadn't been sun. Maybe it was warmed by his hand, though he had just picked it up. Or maybe it kept the heat from his jacket pocket, though the jacket had been on the chair since nine. He noticed each possibility, like catching a faint smell of smoke, then let it go.

He would send a photo to Mark Delano at UMass Dartmouth one of these days. Mark did geology, and Mark owed him a favor from a talk Frank had given at their campus ministry two springs back. Mark could probably tell him in thirty seconds whether it was igneous or metamorphic, which was the category Frank wanted for it, because things in categories behaved.

He put the stone back down. He locked the office.

The hallway from his office to the foyer was thirty-two feet. Frank walked it without counting. There was no reason to count. The fellowship hall smelled of yesterday's coffee and the peculiar resinous warmth pine pews gave off when the heat had been on a while. He shut off the lights as he went.

Outside, the October wind had picked up, and the sound had roughened across the water. The Vineyard was still invisible. Frank pulled his jacket tighter and walked down the crushed-shell drive to his car.

Next week was the Great Awakening. Jonathan Edwards. *Sinners in the Hands of an Angry God.* Another good sermon in him, another chapter in the series. He was already thinking about the opening as he got in the car.

Behind him, the building stood quiet and ordinary. The stone sat on his desk in the dark, and the hallway was thirty-two feet long.

For now.

Chapter 3

Small Anomalies

Tuesday morning. The church was warm. The baseboards had stopped their uneven tapping and kept a steady seventy degrees, and Frank sat at his desk a little after eight with his travel mug, reading *Sinners in the Hands of an Angry God* for the third time in as many days. This time, he made notes in a different color, hoping to see it with new eyes. The move from Cotton Mather to Jonathan Edwards was fifty years and a big change in theology. He wanted the sermon to land like it had the first week. He doubted it would.

The stone sat on the blotter next to the broken stapler, two inches from the edge, where he had left it Sunday afternoon. He did not look at it.

Mid-morning he walked down the hallway to the fellowship hall for more coffee. The women's quilting circle met Tuesday mornings. Six women in their seventies, speaking across a long folding table in the voices New England women used in church basements, patient and conspiratorial. The forty-cup percolator had been running since nine. Frank filled his mug, said something to Marjorie Bento about the weather, nodded at the others, and turned back.

The walk back felt longer.

It wasn't alarming. The hallway hadn't grown or changed in any obvious way. Sometimes a familiar song seems to have an extra beat the first time you notice it, and this felt like that. He noticed it and let it go right away. He'd been at his desk too long. Reading Edwards took stamina. At fifty-two, some mornings just felt a little off.

About a third of the way down the hallway, at roughly the place where he always passed it, hung a framed photograph of the 1978 expansion crew; seven men in overalls, one of them Ray, standing next to a cement mixer. Frank noticed, on this walk, that he had not yet passed the photograph when he should have. Then he passed it. He reached his office. He set the coffee down and opened Edwards to the page he had marked.

The stone was still two inches from the edge of the blotter.

27

• • •

Around eleven a crow flew into the office window. The bird hit the glass with a soft, surprising thud, and Frank looked up in time to see it drop into the rhododendron below the sill. He waited a moment for it to recover. Crows usually did. A minute later it lifted off and disappeared into the pitch pine across the lot. Frank made a small note on his pad to clean the window.

A while later he closed Edwards and took the legal pad and walked back to the fellowship hall to refill his mug. The percolator was off now. The quilters had gone. He poured what was left, lukewarm, into the mug and turned to walk back. He stopped halfway.

He was thinking about the crow. He had heard the impact on the office window. He then realized he'd heard a second thud, almost instantly after the first. The pitch was a little different. The same wall, perhaps the window directly below. He missed it at the time. He remembered it now.

He walked the rest of the hallway to his office. He looked out the window. Nothing on the ground beneath the rhododendron. Nothing on the ground beneath the second window either. The crow had flown off. Maybe its mate had bounced the same glass and flown off too. Maybe he was building a second impact out of his own memory. Maybe the wood in this old building did things to sound. Frank walked back to his office.

• • •

Tuesday evening Frank was in his office catching up on email while the choir rehearsed in the sanctuary. The piano carried through the wall behind him like something half-remembered. Be Thou My Vision, arranged in a key that suited the altos. Linda led the six regulars from the bench. She never left the piano.

Three messages arrived in Frank's inbox. A church leadership newsletter he would not read. A request from a pulpit-supply preacher out of New Bedford for a reference Frank would write tomorrow. And a note from a woman named Helen Bettencourt, who ran the food pantry out of the Baptist church in Mashpee, asking whether Cape Community could commit to a monthly volunteer slot this winter. Fourth Saturday. Two to four hours. They were short, she wrote.

Frank flagged the message and didn't reply. He came up with reasons easily. He needed to talk to the deacons. He needed to check how many volunteers they'd have in November, with the holidays coming. He needed to decide if a Baptist food pantry was the right fit for a non-denominational church's outreach. The reasons made sense, but Frank also knew, even if he didn't say it out loud, that these were the same reasons he'd given Helen the last time she asked, back in March. He hadn't done anything about it then, either.

He flagged this one. He moved on.

At eight-thirty the piano stopped. The choir members said their goodnights in the foyer. A minute later Linda appeared in Frank's open doorway, still in her coat, holding her music folder against her chest. The coat was a man's barn jacket, too big in the shoulders. Her sunglasses were pushed up on her head.

"Frank, weird thing. I went into the choir room to grab the Lord's Supper meditation folder, and I… I couldn't find the light switch."

"Couldn't find it?"

"I mean, I found it. But it wasn't where it usually is. I had to grope around on the opposite wall for a minute. Felt like I was in somebody else's house."

"The wiring in this building is older than I am."

"That's probably it." She laughed, and the laugh did not quite match her face. "Maybe I need glasses."

She waved and went. Her footsteps moved back down the hallway. The side door opened, closed.

Frank looked at the doorway where she had been. He made a note, not about the switch. Linda had not said hello to him on Sunday and had not said hello to him tonight, and the barn jacket was not hers. Frank would not ask about it.

He had known Linda for a decade. He had been in the room with her hundreds of times. He had stood next to her at the piano on Christmas Eves and eaten her peach pie at potlucks and shaken Mike's hand at the front door of the church on the rare Sundays Mike came. Frank had not, in ten years, asked Linda how she was when there was not a piano between them. She came in the back door at nine. She left through the side door before he could catch her in the foyer. He never bothered to interrupt his daily routine to speak with her. He didn't want to find out what Linda would say if he let her speak for three minutes.

The barn jacket was Mike's. Frank was sure of it now. Mike had worn it to the men's breakfast last fall, and Frank had complimented him on it. Mike was a little taller than Linda and broader in the shoulders. Frank only realized

Linda had been wearing her husband's coat for a week or more because she stood in his doorway for those few seconds.

He opened the flagged email from Helen Bettencourt, read it again, closed it without replying, and returned to the sermon.

Several odd things had happened in twelve hours. There were echoing sounds from a crow, a choir-room switch, and a coat that wasn't hers. And there was a small thrum of unease in his chest that wasn't quite fear.

He worked on Edwards until ten.

• • •

Wednesday morning, the sky was a hard, bright blue, typical for October on the Cape. The wind coming off the sound was sharp, hinting that November was near. There were three cars in the church lot: Ray's truck, Jim Souza's van from Souza Mechanical, and Tom's Jeep.

Ray and Jim were in the basement with the furnace, which had been ticking funny for two weeks. Frank could hear, through the heating vents, the particular cadence of two Portuguese men disagreeing about a blower motor. He had stopped trying to follow the content of those conversations years ago. Either the furnace would work or it would not, and Ray would tell him which.

Tom had come in at nine to set up chairs for the potluck and had been setting them up for ninety minutes, which meant he had set up eight chairs and was now sitting in one of them looking at his phone. Around ten-thirty he wandered down the hallway with a styrofoam coffee cup and put his head into Frank's office.

"Pastor Frank. Real quick. I'm telling you, this place is settling."

"Settling."

"Settling settling. I went to plug in the coffeemaker in the fellowship hall, and the outlet is — I swear to God, further from the counter than it was last week. I had to unwind the whole cord. This is how those haunted houses start. I saw it on a thing."

"You saw it on a thing."

"A Netflix thing. Or maybe not Netflix. The point is we should rebrand." Tom smirked. "Historic haunted meetinghouse. Charge twenty bucks a tour. I'd run point."

Frank laughed. Tom grinned again, lifted the coffee cup in a mock toast, and wandered back toward the fellowship hall. He was gone down the hall before the laugh had finished in Frank's throat.

Frank stood. He walked to his office doorway. He looked at the hallway.

Hallway. Choir room. Fellowship hall.

He decided to notice something he'd been ignoring since Sunday. The hallway looked normal. The choir-room door, the small bathroom with the dripping faucet, and the framed photo of the 1978 expansion crew were all in their usual spots. Everything was where it should be. Still, the space between them felt longer than he remembered.

He walked the hallway to the fellowship hall. He counted steps without meaning to. Nineteen. He had made this walk every workday for twenty years. Though he never intentionally counted, he knew the exact number of steps, much like one intuitively understands the rhythm of their own kitchen. Nineteen was wrong. Nineteen was at least three more than it should have been.

He turned around. He walked back to his office. Eighteen. He turned around again. Twenty.

Each time, the number of steps was different, only by one or two, but overall it was more than it should have been. He stood at his office door and felt the small thrum from last night grow a little stronger. It was the kind of ache in the chest that comes when you're about to get bad news.

He went into his office. He sat at the desk. He took the cabinet key off the ring on his desk and opened the small filing cabinet in the corner, and he pulled out the folder of building plans the roofers had borrowed last winter. The roof-project blueprint was on top. The original 1924 architectural drawing, blue ink on yellowed paper, was underneath. He laid the original out on his desk.

He looked at it for a very long minute.

He walked to the supply closet at the far end of the hallway, past the choir room, past the small bathroom where the faucet had a drip nobody had fixed, and he opened it. He grabbed Ray's old steel tape measure from the third shelf, and walked the hallway again with it.

He knelt. He hooked the tape at the baseboard, thumb on the lock. He stood and walked backward, stretching out the tape, watching the numbers roll out beneath his feet. He reached the end of the tape at twenty-five feet. He stopped. He took a yellow sticky note from his pocket, wrote 25 on it, and stuck it to the floor at the tip of the tape hook.

He released the tape, walked forward to his sticky note, and re-anchored at the mark. He let the tape back out toward the fellowship hall. He stopped where the hallway opened into the fellowship hall and read the number at the doorframe.

Twenty-two.

He added it.

Forty-seven feet.

He stood in the hallway holding a steel tape and his head did the thing it always did when a piece of evidence did not fit the frame. It re-checked. He measured again. Forty-seven feet.

He folded the tape measure. He went back to his office.

The filing cabinet sat in the corner by the window. Second drawer. He took out the folder labeled BUILDING 2024 ROOF PROJECT and set it on the desk next to the stone, then opened it. The plans were inside, hand-drawn in blue ink on drafting paper by Michaud Construction of Bourne a year ago, when Joe Michaud measured the building before quoting the roof job. They were based on the 1924 originals and updated for the 1978 expansion.

The hallway dimension was marked in a small, careful hand.

32'.

Joe Michaud's initials next to it. JM.

Frank looked at the plans. He looked at the sticky note still stuck to the floor, visible through his open office door, small and yellow at the edge of his vision. He did not sit down.

He walked back out into the hallway with the tape measure. He anchored again at the foyer end. He measured to his sticky note. Twenty-five feet. He re-anchored. He measured to the fellowship hall doorframe. Twenty-two.

He did it from the other direction. He started at the fellowship hall and walked backward to the foyer.

Forty-seven.

He returned to his office. He put the tape measure on the desk next to the stone. He sat.

He looked at the plans.

The plans could be wrong. They were hand-drawn by a roofing contractor, not an architect. No one had really measured this hallway in a hundred years. The dimension might be a mistake copied from the 1978 drawings, a shortcut, or just a guess.

He picked up his phone and scrolled to Joe Michaud's number. His thumb hovered over the contact as he imagined the call. Joe, this is Frank Silvia at Cape Community. I have a question about the plans you did for the roof job. Is there any chance the main hallway dimension is off? Joe, who was a straightforward man and had always done honest work for the church at a discount, would ask, Off by how much? Frank would answer, Fifteen feet. Joe would be quiet for a few seconds, then gently ask, Frank, are you doing okay?

Frank put the phone down.

He folded the plans and put them back in the folder, then returned the folder to the cabinet. He took the tape measure back to the supply closet at the far end of the hallway, which now seemed farther away than it should have. He walked back to his office and closed the door.

Frank had not closed that door in the middle of the day in twenty years.

• • •

He sat at the desk. The Edwards document was open on the laptop, the cursor blinking where he had left it.

He reached for his coffee mug. His hand brushed the stone.

The stone was not where it had been.

He had left it that morning two inches from the edge of the blotter, near the broken stapler. Now it was touching the stapler, maybe two inches closer to the pen cup than before.

He looked at it. He looked at the door, which was closed. He had not left the office since closing it, except to return the tape measure. Thirty seconds in the hallway. No one had been in this room. Nobody had a key except him and Ray, and Ray had left at eleven.

He thought a bit.

He was a fidgeter. He turned his mug while he read and moved his paperweight when he paused mid-sentence. He had almost certainly picked up the stone while thinking about Edwards, set it down in the wrong spot, and forgotten.

Almost certainly.

He slid the stone back toward the edge of the blotter. As he moved it, he noticed for the first time that the felt beneath it had a mark, a faint oval impression slightly darker than the surrounding blotter, where the stone had been sitting since Sunday afternoon. The oval was empty now. The stone fit back into it exactly.

He looked at the impression for a long moment.

Then he opened Edwards.

• • •

Around three the lights in his office flickered. Once, twice, then steady. He glanced up and waited for them to flicker again, because old wiring in old buildings flickered all the time. Then his desk lamp went out by itself. He reached for the switch and the lamp came back on at his touch without him having clicked it.

He sat with his hand on the switch for a moment. Then he turned the lamp off himself, deliberately, and turned it back on, and it worked the way a lamp was supposed to work.

He left the lamp on.

• • •

A little after five, a knock at the door. Frank had not noticed that two hours had passed, that the light through the window had gone from afternoon to the flat blue of New England dusk, that the sanctuary had cooled behind him. He opened the door. Megan was in the hallway with a stapled spreadsheet in her hand.

"Hey. You got a minute? Sound system."

"Come in."

She came in. She set the spreadsheet on the desk, and she set it down directly next to the tape measure and the stone and the closed Edwards document, and Frank watched her do this and she did not look at any of it. She flipped to page two.

"The Shure wireless handhelds are toast. Both of them cut out Sunday. You didn't hear it because you were preaching. I put together a quote. Seven hundred and twelve dollars for a two-handheld set with a new receiver. The breakdown's on page three."

"Can you show me."

She showed him. She was good at this. She had done comparison pricing in three columns, new, refurbished, and the same set off eBay, each with pros and cons in a smaller font beneath. She had noted that the tech-upgrade line item had been zeroed by Ray in June, so the money would have to come from somewhere else. She said she had already talked to Jim at the bank about what the general fund looked like this month, which Frank had not asked her to do.

"I'll talk to Red," he said.

"Okay."

She did not move to leave. She straightened up and looked at him for a beat that was longer than a beat usually was with Megan, who did not generally hold eye contact with adults unless she was waiting on a setting check.

"Pastor."

"Yeah."

"Three years I've been at the booth."

"I know."

"Three years and what I've asked you for, in dollars, total, is about nine hundred and fifty. I'm asking now for seven hundred and twelve more. I've never asked for a raise. I work for Tuesday-night pizza." She paused. He could not read her expression. "I'm not — I'm not complaining. That's not what this is. I'm just saying. The mics matter. People can't hear the sermon if I don't have working mics. And the sermons are — the sermons matter to you. Right?"

"Of course they matter to me."

"Then we should fix the mics."

"Megan, I said I'd talk to Red."

"Yeah." A small nod. The kind of nod she gave to a setting that almost worked. "Okay."

Her eyes passed over the desk. They stopped on the stone.

"Where'd you get that?"

"Salem. A ledge near the execution site. I was up there Saturday for research."

"Huh."

She picked it up. She turned it over in her fingers, once, slow, the way she handled a cable she was checking for a short. The quartz vein caught the light.

"It's warm."

She said it the way she said ready at the board on Sunday mornings. Without inflection. An observation. The coffee is cold. The input is clipping. It's warm.

She set the stone back into its oval. She tucked the spreadsheet under her arm.

"Let me know about the mics. Ray's easier to convince if you bring him donuts."

She left.

Her footsteps moved down the hallway. The hallway that was forty-seven feet long. The footsteps took longer than they should have. Frank began counting, and he did not mean to be counting, and he lost track somewhere past forty and Megan was still walking. Then the front door of the church opened and closed, and the hallway went quiet.

He sat down.

He placed his hand on the stone. It felt hot, warmer than it had been on Sunday. He kept it there for a moment. He glanced at the cabinet with the plans, but he still couldn't quite make sense of it all.

Still, the connection was trying to form. It hovered at the edge of his mind, like a word you almost remember but can't say, or something you once knew but can't quite reach.

Outside, a car pulled into the crushed-shell lot. Then another.

The first of the potluck regulars.

Chapter 4

Wednesday Potluck

A little before six, Frank got up from his desk and put on his jacket. The stone was still in his right pocket, where he had dropped it earlier without thinking. He left his office and walked down the hallway.

The hallway still felt too long. He walked it without keeping track of his steps.

The fellowship hall was warm, the warmest place in the building on a potluck Wednesday. The forty-cup percolator had been hissing since five, the oven was on for Grace's casserole, and twenty people filled the room with a heat the old baseboards could never match on their best day. Frank hung his jacket on the hook by the door, just like always, and stepped into a room that already smelled like tuna noodle, weak coffee, and the faint sweet char of a pie the Youngs had left in the oven a little too long.

Grace's casserole sat in its familiar Corningware, the same one she'd brought since 1989. She stood at the end of the center table, setting out paper plates, already planning to handle cleanup. Joanne Medeiros brought a foil tray of ziti, its corner dented from the drive, and her two kids, nine and twelve, were at the far end of the table, drifting toward a tablet. Ray brought a store-bought apple pie from Shaws in Falmouth and two gallons of cider. He thought baking was a waste of time, and no one ever disagreed. Tom brought a bag of potato chips. Paul and Marjorie Bento arrived with their usual Jell-O mold, orange this time, which would go uneaten, as it had since the Reagan years. The Monteiros, the retired couple from third row left on Sundays, brought a Pyrex of green bean casserole. Dave or Dan—Frank still wasn't sure which—brought cookies from the fancy bakery on Main Street, and most were already gone.

Linda arrived empty-handed. She apologized to Grace at the door, saying she'd had a hard day and couldn't make it to the store. Grace touched her arm and told her there was plenty. Linda took a paper plate with half a roll and went to the end of the room by the piano, where a couple of folding chairs faced the food tables. She sat down. She didn't play the piano; it was always covered with a sheet on Wednesdays.

The Cabrals were not there. They were traveling, Florida, back on Sunday.

Megan was in the corner near the tablet, plate on her knees, scrolling her phone. She had said she would stay for Ray's announcements. Ray always did the treasurer's update at Wednesday meetings, and he liked having a mic for it even when the room was small, and Megan liked anything that involved gear. She ate ziti with a plastic fork and said nothing.

There were about twenty people. Frank found himself counting, even though he hadn't meant to. Tonight, he kept track.

Ray sat at the center table, telling a story about a guy in a Range Rover at Falmouth Plaza who couldn't figure out how to back out of a parking spot. The story didn't really go anywhere, but that was fine. Paul Bento reported that the bluefish were running late this year. Nobody followed up on the bluefish. Tom, mid-bite, said something about the Patriots that triggered three minutes of discussion that clarified nothing and ended with Dave-or-Dan saying yeah, next year.

Joanne's nine-year-old, a dark-haired kid named Eli, slid up to Frank with a paper plate of cookies balanced on his forearm.

"Pastor Frank. Can God make a rock He can't lift?"

"Philosophers have been arguing about that one for about a thousand years."

"Yeah ok, but whatda you think?"

"I think it's a better question than most of the ones I hear on a Wednesday."

Eli was not satisfied. He took his cookies and went back to his brother.

• • •

At seven, Ray stood up and clapped his hands together twice. He had been doing this for twenty-two years. It was the signal. Plates went down. The room quieted.

Ray read the prayer list off a printout. Most of it was lifted from Sunday's bulletin. One update, delivered with a small nod of satisfaction. Betty Sullivan was out of rehab and home, recovering nicely. There was a ripple of approval. Ray added that the mission envelopes were still available in the foyer and that a few people had not turned theirs in. This too was delivered with a nod, a different kind.

Frank prayed. The prayer was serviceable and warm and hit all the notes he had been trained to hit. He asked God to be with Betty in her recovery. He asked for traveling mercies for the Cabrals. He asked for the missionaries in East Asia by the first names on the prayer card. He said in Jesus' Name. The room said amen.

Grace prayed next. Grace's prayer was longer than Frank's and sounded less like a prayer than a conversation Grace was having with someone she knew better than she knew most of the people in the room. She prayed for Betty. She prayed for the family on Route 151 whose house had burned last month, Lord You know their names if we don't. She prayed for Linda, gently and without specifics, and Linda did not look up. Then Grace said, in the same voice:

"And Lord, make us people who do and not just people who say. In Jesus' name. Amen."

The room echoed with 'amen.' A few more people prayed. Then Ray stepped up and gave his treasurer's update. It took ninety seconds and focused on the furnace. No one asked any questions—no one ever did, and that was just how Ray liked it.

The meeting transitioned into dessert and more coffee. Megan looked up from her phone once during Grace's prayer and then back down. The pie came out. The kids returned to the tablet.

• • •

At eight-thirty, Marjorie Bento got up and started gathering the Jell-O mold. No one had touched it, so she would take it home in the same bowl she brought. Paul picked up the cider jug next. The Monteiros left soon after, since Pat Monteiro had an early appointment in Hyannis and needed to leave. Saying goodnight took about ten minutes, which was about average.

At eight forty-five, Marjorie arrived at the front door of the fellowship hall. She balanced the Jell-O bowl on one hip and used her free hand to open the door.

She paused not going in.

For about three seconds, she stayed quiet, which was unusual for Marjorie Bento. Then she spoke:

"That's not right."

Paul came up behind her with the cider. He looked past her shoulder into the doorway.

"Did they do renovations?"

Tom was halfway into his jacket when he wandered over, as he often did with anything that caught his attention. He looked down past Marjorie.

"Oh… that's weird."

He spoke as if he were just mentioning a burned-out light. No one was alarmed yet.

Beyond the doorway, a hallway stretched out. It was long, lit by fluorescent tubes overhead. Pine baseboards lined the walls, but Frank didn't recognize their style. The hallway was painted the same beige as the rest of the church, yet it ran in a direction the building shouldn't have, and it was longer than the church was wide. Doors appeared at intervals along the hall, but none of them seemed to fit.

Ray stepped up behind Tom and looked.

Ray had spent forty years working construction on the Cape. He had hung drywall in every kind of New England building that needed it. He had gone over the plans for this church four times. Ray stared down the hallway for about ten seconds, which was a long time for him, then said quietly:

"Close it."

Marjorie closed the door. It clicked shut. Behind them, the fellowship hall had grown quiet, though no one could say exactly when.

Ray went to the side door by the fellowship hall, the one that led to the parking lot. He moved a bit faster than usual, but not quite hurrying. He opened the door.

He did not step through.

On the other side of the door was a small room, maybe eight by ten feet. A single fluorescent tube in the ceiling flickered like it was about to burn out. The floor was wooden. There were no windows, no other doors, and no furniture.

It was a room that didn't belong in this building and had never been there before.

Ray closed the door. He shut it carefully, almost as if he didn't want to, as if something on the other side might be watching him.

At the far end of the fellowship hall, Tom was already at the back emergency exit, under the red EXIT sign that had glowed since 1987. The kitchen was to the right. Tom pushed the crash bar and the door opened.

"Oh," Tom said. And then, quieter, "What the…?"

Beyond the emergency exit was a staircase made of pine, with handrails on both sides. They looked like the basement stairs you'd find in any New England building from 1924. The stairs went down so far that Frank, across the room, couldn't see where they ended.

Cape Community Church didn't have a basement. The furnace was in a crawl space you could only reach from outside. The building sat on a slab poured in 1924 and reinforced in 1978. There had never been a basement or a staircase.

"Nobody," Ray said, his voice loud enough for everyone to hear, but with a hint of fear. "Go down those stairs. Nobody."

Pat Monteiro, standing near the food table, says, "What, what's going on?"

"I don't know. I don't know what's going on." Tom replied.

Dave or Dan asked, reasonably, about the front door. The main entrance. The big wooden door with the handrail Ray had installed three winters back.

Two people walked to the foyer to check. Frank was one of them. The foyer still looked like the foyer. The bulletin board was still there. The missions envelopes were still in their little wooden box next to the guest book. The front door was still the front door.

Frank opened it.

The front door opened onto a hallway.

This wasn't the same hallway that had been behind Marjorie's door. It was a different one, running perpendicular to the first. Both hallways seemed to lead toward the parking lot, even though the lot was only on one side of the building. As Frank stood in the doorway, holding the knob, he felt his sense of space twist in a way that didn't make sense.

Megan appeared at his elbow, coming from the booth without making a sound. She looked past him at the hallway.

"That's not — okay, no. No. That's — the geometry doesn't work."

She muttered it quietly, almost to herself, but Frank heard her. The geometry doesn't work. After three years running the sound board, Megan always described things in physical terms first. The geometry didn't work. Frank closed the door.

He turned to go back to the fellowship hall, and Megan was already moving past him to check the side door of the sanctuary.

Dave or Dan took out his phone and tried to call someone. There was no service, even though it had worked ten minutes earlier. The Wi-Fi still worked. Megan in the booth had been streaming music just five minutes ago, but the cell network was gone. Tom checked his phone and watched as two bars dropped to one, then to none.

Joanne pulled her phone out of her back pocket. She had the same problem. She tried calling her mother in Bourne, but nothing happened.

Tom said the Wi-Fi was still working, so someone could try sending a text that way. Joanne gave it a shot, but the message didn't go through. Her phone showed 'delivering' for thirty seconds, then 'not delivered' in red letters under the message bubble.

"Okay," Marjorie said. She set the Jell-O mold on a folding chair by the door. She spoke in the calm voice she used with her grandchildren. "Let's not panic, all right. Let's just go to the parking lot. Out the front. Let's all go outside."

Ray was already at the front door. He had opened it. He was looking at the same hallway Frank had just looked at. He closed it again, quietly. He turned to the room.

"There's no parking lot through the front door right now."

Pat Monteiro suggested, "Try the side."

Ray walked to the side door of the fellowship hall, the one he had opened five minutes ago, the one that had shown him a small empty room. He opened it.

The room was still there.

He closed it and walked to the kitchen door, the small service entrance the janitors used. He opened it. There was a corridor, lit and empty, running in a direction the building wasn't supposed to have.

He closed it.

He came back to the room.

"Nobody," he said again, slower this time, "leave the building through any door without checking with me first."

He looked over at Frank for a moment. He was not asking for advice, just seeing if the man in charge of the building had anything to say, like someone who knows the place well might.

Frank did not have anything to add.

Dave or Dan was already at the nearest window, a tall double-hung in the east wall of the fellowship hall, the kind that had been opened every August for thirty years to let the heat out. He flipped the lock. He pushed up on the lower sash.

The sash did not move.

He pressed his palms against the rail and pushed with his shoulders. Nothing happened. It wasn't stuck like a window in humid weather, when the wood swells. The sash just wouldn't move. He tried the next window with the same result, and then the one behind the food table. Still nothing.

Pat Monteiro picked up a folding chair by its back and walked to the window beside the piano. He looked at Ray, who nodded. Pat swung the chair hard against the lower pane. The leg of the chair hit with a sound that should have been glass breaking, but it wasn't. Instead, it was a dull, flat sound, as if the window had turned to stone at the moment of impact. The chair bounced back. Pat looked at the leg, now dented, then at the window, which didn't have a single mark.

He set the chair down.

"It's not glass…anymore," he said.

Frank went to the window by the foyer door and pressed his palm against it. It felt cold, just like glass. He could see the parking lot, his Camry, the pitch pine across the lot, and the gray October dusk. Everything outside looked normal. The world was still there, but the window wouldn't let them through.

He took his hand off the glass.

"The windows aren't an option," he said.

It was, he realized, the first thing he had said since Marjorie had opened the connector door.

Dave or Dan was beside him now. Frank did not know the man's first name, did not know the man's last name, had been greeting him with a generic morning for two years. The man was looking at the unbreakable window with the same expression Frank had seen on his face in the foyer every Sunday, the friendly readiness of a person who showed up and was never quite asked to do more than that.

Frank turned to him.

"I'm sorry. I have to ask you something I should have asked a long time ago."

The man looked at him.

"What's your name?"

There was a pause. The man's face stayed almost the same, but his shoulders shifted slightly. He spoke in a flat voice, as if he had answered this question many times before.

"Dave. Dave Fernandes."

"Dave," Frank said. He met the man's eyes for a moment longer than needed. "I'm sorry it took me this long."

Dave gave him a small nod. He didn't let Frank off the hook, but he accepted the apology and turned back to the window. The window was the bigger problem now, and there would be time for everything else if they got out.

Frank felt the stone in his pocket flare up. It didn't hurt. It was like a coal in a fire glow brighter when someone finally added the right piece of kindling.

• • •

Nobody called the meeting to order, but within a minute the congregation drifted back into the fellowship hall and gathered around the center table with the dishes. The potluck food was still out, the coffee was still warm, and Marjorie's Jell-O mold was starting to slump in its bowl, the orange turning glossy under the lights.

Twenty people. Standing in a room. Looking at each other.

Ray cleared his throat. "Okay. Nobody panic. There's got to be an explanation." He told himself it had to be something with the boiler. Maybe a gas leak, or CO2. Something like that.

He said it because he felt he should, not because he really believed it. He kept holding his phone.

Tom let out a laugh, but it sounded wrong. He laughed only because he didn't know what else to do. "Historic haunted meetinghouse," he said. No one else joined in. His face fell, and he stopped talking.

Grace stood up from her chair at the end of the table and closed the Bible on her lap. She looked around the room, steady and calm. After forty-three years in this building, she had never felt afraid here before. "I think we should pray."

Frank was the pastor. Leading this room was his job. Suddenly, he realized the words he'd learned for moments like this wouldn't be enough. He started to speak, then stopped.

Megan stood in the doorway between the foyer and the fellowship hall. She hadn't moved since she said the geometry didn't work. Her phone hung loosely at her side as she watched the adults, the way she often did on Sundays. Frank felt the pressure of being watched by a teenager who seemed more present than he was.

Eli Medeiros, the nine-year-old, started to cry. Quietly. Joanne pulled him against her.

Nobody said a thing.

• • •

Frank stood near the center of the room, not quite between the food table and the seats, with his congregation looking at him. He had no idea what to do. Deep down, he knew this was a reckoning he had put off for years.

His hand moved before he thought about it. It was a nervous habit he'd had for four days. His right hand slipped into the right pocket of his jacket—the one he'd worn to Salem and every day this week, with keys in the left pocket and the stone in the right. His fingers closed around the stone.

The stone was hot. Not just warm, but truly hot. There was nothing to see, no glow or pulse, nothing he could show or explain to anyone else. It was just heat, like holding a mug of coffee straight from the microwave, burning against his palm.

Frank stood in the middle of the fellowship hall while his congregation watched him. His phone sat useless in one pocket, and his hand was wrapped around a stone he had picked up behind a Walgreens in Salem four days earlier. Now, he finally understood what the stone was doing.

He did not say anything.

Part Two

The Labyrinth

Chapter 5

Mapping the Impossible

The silence stretched until it felt awkward, and then it lingered. The stone stayed hot. Frank's congregation kept their eyes on him.

Ray cleared his throat.

Ray wasn't a fan of public speaking, but after forty years on job sites, he knew what to do when things got dangerous. If a roof was about to give way, someone had to speak up and get everyone out. Ray had done that more times than he could remember. He did it again now.

"All right. Here's what we're gonna do. Nobody goes off alone. We're going to check every exit in this building, one by one. We pair up. Thirty minutes. Then we meet back here and try to figure out what's goin' on."

The room responded. Not because Ray was inspiring, but because Ray was doing something while everyone else was trying not to panic, and that gave him authority.

Frank watched Ray take charge and felt something he hadn't felt in twenty years at this church: out of place. He was the pastor. This was his building. The congregation looked at Ray because Ray was doing something, and Frank wasn't.

He pulled his hand from his pocket. The stone had left a mark on his palm, a faint red spot where his fingers had gripped it.

Ray assigned pairs. He put himself with Tom and gave them the back emergency exit, because Ray wanted to look at those stairs again. He paired Grace with Marjorie. Dave with Paul Bento. The Youngs together. Joanne stayed with the kids.

Frank was paired with Megan. Megan already had her phone out, a notes app open, a list of exits being documented.

• • •

Megan led. She walked to the side door of the fellowship hall, the one Ray had opened twenty minutes earlier, the one that had shown him a room.

The room was still there.

The room was eight by ten feet, with a flickering fluorescent light overhead, bare wood floor, beige walls, no windows, and no other doors. Megan stepped inside. Frank didn't. She walked around the edge, pressing her hand to each wall and tapping with her knuckles. The walls sounded solid. She reached the door they had entered through and stood in the doorway. The fellowship hall was still there, just as it had been. She stepped back into the fellowship hall. She closed the door. She opened it again.

The room was still there.

"Not an illusion," she said. "It's a real room."

She took a photo with her phone. The shutter clicked. She checked her camera roll. The photo was there, clear—a small beige room with a flickering fluorescent light. She showed Frank the screen without saying anything. Frank nodded.

They went to the kitchen. The small service door at the back was the janitor's door. Frank had walked through it hundreds of times in twenty years, out to the dumpster and back, and knew its sticky bottom hinge and how it needed a shove if your hands were full. He opened it now. It didn't stick.

It opened onto a corridor.

It was lit from a source Frank couldn't find. There were no overhead lights and no windows, just pale, even light from somewhere unseen. Pine floor. Beige walls. The corridor stretched forward with no end in sight.

Megan counted her steps as she walked in. Twelve. Twenty. Thirty. At forty, she stopped and turned around.

Frank stood in the doorway, not moving. Megan returned, counting forty steps like before, and walked past him into the kitchen.

"The size is way off," she said, her voice flat and clinical, the way she sounded when something needed measuring. "I'm gonna map this."

She took a photo of the corridor. The shutter clicked. She took another from a different angle, with the kitchen tile at the bottom for scale. She checked her camera roll. Both photos had saved. She showed Frank.

"Okay," Megan said. "One more."

They checked the sanctuary side door. It opened into another hallway. This hallway turned left at the far end and disappeared around a corner where the outside wall should have been. Megan took a photo of the turn but didn't step inside. Frank stayed back too. He realized he hadn't crossed any thresholds in the last twenty-five minutes, and he wasn't about to start now.

They walked back to the fellowship hall.

Everyone gathered again at the center tables. The dishes were still out, untouched. Grace began tossing used plates, because she couldn't stand being in a messy room and had to do something about it. Meanwhile, the food was slowly making its way, one pan at a time, into the kitchen fridge.

Eli Medeiros slept across two folding chairs, with Joanne's coat covering him. His older brother sat with the tablet, but it was off; he just stared at the blank screen. Someone had restarted the coffee in the urn. The fellowship hall had that stuffy smell buildings get when no one opens a door for hours.

Ray stood at the head of the table and walked around, his voice echoing a little as he asked everyone for their reports.

Ray and Tom went down the back stairs. They counted at least a hundred steps before Ray told Tom to stop, but they still hadn't reached the bottom. The pine-paneled walls matched the original 1924 interior, and there was no dust on the handrails. Ray pointed this out, noticing details most pastors missed.

Dave and Paul stood at the front door. The hallway stretched straight for sixty steps before splitting into a T. The left side ended at a door leading to another hallway, while the right side ended at a door that opened into a chapel.

"Not our chapel," Paul said. "It's smaller, older, with box pews. Looks like something from Plymouth."

No one knew what to say to that, so Ray continued.

Grace and Marjorie had stood by the connector door. The hallway stretched for about two hundred steps; Grace had counted. Doors lined the walls at regular intervals. Marjorie tried three of them: one was locked, one seemed to be a classroom, and one opened onto a linen closet filled with folded towels and the smell of cedar.

The Youngs waited by the kitchen service door. A stairwell led upward to a landing and another door. They had not opened that second door yet. Ray nodded slowly.

"Alright," he said. "That's good. Only open doors if you need to."

Megan and Frank talked about the three doors Megan had just taken pictures of.

The reports added up to something no one wanted to mention. Paul Bento, a lobster boat captain for thirty-two years who spoke plainly, was the first to say it.

"The building is bigger on the inside than the outside."

Megan was already spreading a bulletin flat on the table. "Yeah," she said. "That's what I'm writing down."

• • •

She took a pen from the basket on the welcome table, smoothed the paper with her hand, and started to draw. The original church went in first. Fellowship hall as a rectangle in the center. Foyer. Sanctuary. Kitchen. Frank's office at the end of the long hallway. Choir room. The small bathroom with the drip. The supply closet. She drew it to rough scale, and it fit on a space about the size of a dinner plate.

Then she added the new parts they had discovered.

She drew the back staircase as an arrow going down from the kitchen wall and wrote next to it: 100+ steps, no bottom. She drew the corridor from the kitchen service door as a line running north, labeled 40+ steps, end unseen. She sketched the hallway off the foyer, the T-junction, and the colonial chapel as a small square with PEWS, 1700s? written beside it. The two-hundred-step hallway from the connector door became a bold line with tick marks for each door —one circled for the locked one, another marked classroom, another linen closet. The small room off the fellowship hall side door was a dead-end box.

When she finished, the original church sat in the middle, with the impossible building stretching out in every direction. Even as a rough estimate, the new parts were many times larger than the church itself.

She pushed the map to the center of the table.

Tom wandered over. He had been quiet for twenty minutes, which was a record for Tom. He stared at the map for a long time.

"Kid," he said, "you should be an engineer."

Megan didn't look up. "I been thinkin' about it."

Grace sat at the next table with the Bible open on her lap again. She studied the map with the same quiet focus she had when she watched Linda play piano, as if she was used to paying attention even when no one expected it.

Megan put the cap back on the pen, stepped back from the map, and looked at it.

"The building is bigger on the inside than the outside," she said, repeating Paul's words. "That's not a structural problem. It's something totally different."

Nobody answered. As the words settled in the silent room, it felt as though time itself had stopped.

Frank watched Megan step back from the map and realized again what he'd noticed when Ray started assigning pairs. A seventeen-year-old was doing the kind of thinking that, by any normal measure, should have been his job. He was trained for a different kind of problem. He had no training for this.

He walked away from the table. Not far. To the doorway between the fellowship hall and the short connector to the foyer, the door Marjorie had opened at eight forty-five.

He opened it.

The hallway was still there. Lit. Waiting.

Frank studied the hallway as carefully as he would a rare manuscript at the Peabody Essex, focused and detached. The baseboards were pine, like those in the church, but less worn, as if no one had touched them with a mop in a century. The trim matched the style of the 1920s. The ceiling was eight feet high, just like the rest of the building. The fluorescent tubes above were older than those in the original church. They weren't broken, just from a different time, casting a different shade of white.

The hallway was not hostile. It was simply, undeniably, there.

He had the thought, clearly and almost academically, that this was interesting.

Then another thought followed: interesting was the wrong reaction for a pastor facing something impossible, with his congregation waiting behind him for answers he didn't have.

He closed the door.

When he turned back to the room, Megan was watching him. She had seen him stand at the threshold. She had seen him not step through. Her face did not change. She went back to the map.

• • •

Around midnight, Tom went missing.

Not far, and not for long. Joanne noticed first. She always kept track of everyone in the room when children were around. She called Tom's name. Ray looked up from his map. The Youngs looked up too. Linda, sitting by the piano, did not.

Four minutes later Tom walked back in through the connector door, a Sharpie in one hand and a half-guilty grin on his face. He looked pleased with himself, the way he always did when he'd done something he probably shouldn't have.

"Okay," he said. "I know, Red, nobody goes alone. I know. I know. Just hear me out."

Ray's face changed color in an instant.

"Tom," he said, clearly upset.

"I… I wanted to see if it was the same hallway. If you walk in and back out. So I went in, fifty steps, I marked the wall. Small X. Right side. Eye height, used a Sharpie. Then I walked back out. I'm fine. See. I'm right here," he said, smiling. "But I want to check out something."

He was already moving to the door. Ray started to tell him to stop. Tom opened the door and stepped through.

Ray went in after him. Frank went after Ray. Megan went after Frank, the map rolled in her hand, her phone out.

Fifty steps into the hallway and Tom stopped.

The X was not there.

And the wall where Tom had drawn the X was not there either. In its place, a new hallway branched off to the right. Pine floor. Beige walls. The same light as the main corridor. Running perpendicular into a distance neither of them could see the end of.

Tom stood staring for a long second.

"It was right here. I was right here. I drew the X."

"I believe you," Ray said.

"There was a wall right here," Tom said, his voice firm even though he still wasn't sure what he was seeing.

Megan photographed the new branch. The shutter clicked. She made a note on her bulletin map. She looked at Tom.

"It moved," she said. "Or it grew. The hallway responded to you."

Tom's face lost some color. He kept holding the Sharpie and looked at it like it had betrayed him.

"Back," Ray said. "Back. Back to the room. Now!"

They went back. Fifty steps to the connector door, which was where it had been. Through it. Into the fellowship hall.

Twenty heads turned.

Ray held up a hand before Tom could speak.

"It moved," Ray said. "The building moves when you're in it. Don't go in unless you have to."

• • •

A little after one, Frank returned to the connector door leading to the strange hallway. He placed his hand on the knob but didn't open it.

Behind him, Joanne had gotten Eli's brother to lie down. Ray was at the map with Megan. Linda was on the bench with her eyes closed. Grace was in the kitchen organizing carefully arranging the leftover food in the refrigerator. She worked with the focus of someone who had survived three husbands and four hospital stays by always keeping track of what she had.

Frank was thinking about Salem. He remembered picking up a stone at the base of a granite outcrop. His hand had been warm, and so had the stone, but he hadn't wondered why. He thought about the woman on the park bench. He thought about Helen Bettencourt's email, which he had flagged but not answered. He thought about Linda's barn jacket, which belonged to Mike, and how Linda had worn it in his office on Tuesday night because something had gone wrong at her house, and he hadn't asked.

The night continued. Frank kept his hand on the knob and lingered at the doorway, standing between the part of the building where he had built his ministry and the part that existed because he had not.

56

Chapter 6

Fractures

Grace restarted the coffee before dawn. Someone—maybe Grace—had wiped the tables. The dishes were in the kitchen. Grace spent about an hour reorganizing the pantry, not because it needed it, but because it was the only work left.

When Grace finished, she sat at the end of the center table with her leather Bible on her lap. The tabs stuck out, just as they always did. Frank, sitting across the room, could tell which book she had opened. Titus was near the back, a short book, and it had always been one of Grace's favorites.

She didn't read to herself. Instead, she used the same voice she used for prayer. It was not loud, but clear enough for everyone to hear. The room was so quiet that every word carried.

"They profess to know God, but they deny him by their works. They are detestable, disobedient, unfit for any good work." She read it once, then closed the Bible.

Nobody asked her what she was reading. No one asked her why, either.

Ray sat at the map table, his heavy-lidded, bloodshot eyes making it clear he had only slept for ninety minutes in a folding chair. A cold Dunkin' cup rested by his elbow. He picked it up twice in five minutes but never took a sip. Tom went to the kitchen twice, once for peanut butter on stale bread and once for more coffee.

Linda had not moved from the piano end of the room since last night. She had not played or spoken since dinner. At some point, Grace brought her a sleeve of Saltines. Linda ate two and set the rest on top of the piano.

Joanne woke the boys. Grace discovered an unopened box of Cheerios in a cabinet that nobody remembered filling. The boys sat by the wall, eating dry cereal straight from the box with their hands. Eli's older brother held the tablet on his lap, but its battery was dead.

Megan sat on a folding chair against the wall, phone in hand. She scrolled through her camera roll, pausing on a photo of the small, impossible room. She zoomed in, let go, then zoomed in again, searching for something she still hadn't found.

Frank had planted himself by one of the fellowship-hall windows. He had returned to that spot again and again over the past two hours. His right hand stayed in his pocket, the stone hot against his palm.

Brian and Ellen Young sat alone at a table, their heads close together. Brian's Bible was open in front of him.

The Bentos were in the corner. Paul had a deck of cards from his jacket pocket and was playing solitaire on a cleared table edge. Marjorie sat opposite him, her knitting resting idly in her lap, untouched.

The building looked the same as it had at midnight. There were no new hallways, and the doors stayed where they were. After thirty-one hours, the silence felt deeply unsettling.

A little after nine, Brian Young stood up from his table. At thirty-two, he worked in administration at the Woods Hole Oceanographic Institution. For the past six months, he had been coming to Cape Community, holding onto the hope people feel when they think they have finally found what they want. He walked over to the map, still holding his Bible.

"Red. I was thinking. Maybe we should stop trying to figure it out and, you know, pray. All of us together. The Lord shows people the way out."

Ray looked up from the map. He had framed houses in every town on the Upper Cape, and after forty years of that work, he knew how to deal with fatigue the way you deal with a bad hip. You don't complain. You just push through. But this morning, that wasn't working.

"Brian. We've been praying. Grace has been praying since eleven last night. I've been praying. Frank's been praying."

He paused. Brian opened his mouth. Ray was not done.

"Whatever is doing this, praying hasn't stopped it." Ray pressed his thumb and forefinger into the corners of his eyes. "God doesn't seem to be answering the phone this morning."

Ray wished he hadn't said it the moment the words left his mouth. Frank noticed, but Ray didn't try to take it back.

Brian's face fell. He didn't argue. He stepped back and said quietly, "I'll pray by myself, then," before returning to Ellen.

Grace, in the kitchen, pretended she hadn't heard. She picked up a can of cream of mushroom soup and turned the label to the front of the shelf.

The room was quieter than it had been.

By eleven, Pat Monteiro sat at a table with Paul Bento. At first, they spoke quietly about what they thought was happening. Pat had worked as a dentist in Falmouth for decades and liked to solve problems by getting more technical as he explained them. Paul used to be a lobster captain out of New Bedford until his knees gave out. He was the kind of Cape Cod Portuguese former Catholic who believed in things you couldn't see, but he found most conversations about them awkward.

"Gas leak," Pat said with confidence. "There was a case in Connecticut in the eighties. A family of four all saw the same apparitions for two weeks. Cracked heat exchanger. Carbon monoxide at the wrong level can cause vivid shared hallucinations. That's not speculation, it's documented. Neurological. The furnace has been making odd noises for two weeks. Red said so himself."

"It doesn't explain the photographs," Paul said.

"It's that mass hysteria and confirmation bias thing. They look at the photograph and see what everyone else saw."

"Pat. I saw the photograph. The photograph shows a room that is not in this building."

"You think it shows that."

Marjorie set her coffee down. "It's spiritual, Pat. Don't be a fool."

"Marjorie. With all due respect. That is not a theory. That is ignoring the problem."

"It is a diagnosis, Patrick. You're the one ignoring things."

Dave cleared his throat. "What if somebody's filming us? Like a prank show — kinda like the Truman Show."

No one answered him. Paul slowly moved his coffee cup around on the table in circles. After a quiet pause, he said, "There hasn't been a prank show on Cape Cod in fifty years."

Pat pressed Marjorie again, and Marjorie's patience wore thin. Paul stepped in to mediate, careful as if he were moving between shelves of fragile glassware in a small shop. On the other side of the room, Ellen Young began to cry quietly, covering her mouth with one hand. Brian gently put his arm around her.

Joanne looked up from the Cheerios on the floor.

"Hey," she said. "Guys. Not in front of them please."

The argument stopped, but nothing was resolved. Pat went back to his coffee, jaw set. Marjorie returned to her knitting. Dave wandered off. Paul gathered the cards and started playing solitaire again.

• • •

Around two, Linda got up from the piano bench. She whispered something to Grace—the first words anyone had heard from her in ten hours—then left the hall and walked into the main church hall. Not the unfamiliar hallways, but the original one, heading toward the small bathroom near Frank's office.

She didn't return after ten minutes. Then fifteen passed.

Tom noticed. He'd been on edge since the Sharpie incident and had quietly decided to be more helpful today, so he stood up and went to look for her.

Frank came in a minute later. He had felt uneasy ever since Ray snapped at Brian, and he knew he still hadn't done any real 'pastor work' today.

Tom found her first. When Frank turned the corner from the fellowship hall, he saw Linda sitting on the hallway floor, halfway between the choir room and the bathroom. Her back was against the wall, knees drawn up, and her palms pressed flat on the floor on either side of her, as if she was making sure the floor was still there. She was hyperventilating.

Tom stood about ten feet away, shifting his hands in and out of his pockets. He wasn't sure what to do with them.

"Linda. Hey. You — hey. You okay?"

She shook her head.

"You want water? I can get Grace. I can get someone."

She shook her head again. Her breathing was loud and uneven.

Tom didn't move. Frank could see that he was unsure what to do next. Even though Tom had spent eleven years as a youth pastor, he had never dealt with something like this with an adult. He was used to helping teenagers, but facing someone he respected was different. He wasn't sure he could handle it.

Frank stepped past Tom. Moments like this were supposed to be familiar to a pastor. He tried to remember what he had learned.

"Linda. I want you to breathe with me. In through your nose for four counts. Hold for seven. Out through your mouth for eight. Four, seven, eight. Can you try that?"

This was the right protocol. He'd learned it from a pastoral care manual and even remembered the name of the technique.

He gave the instructions while standing, from across the hallway. He didn't kneel beside her or put a hand on her shoulder. He didn't ask what happened in the bathroom. He offered pastoral care the way he gave a sermon: with the right words, but at a distance.

After a while, Linda's breathing slowed—not because of Frank, but because panic attacks eventually end. She lifted her hands from the floor, wiped her face with the back of her hand, stood up without looking at either of them, and walked back toward the fellowship hall.

Grace was in the hallway. Frank didn't know how long she'd been there. She came around the corner, quiet and steady, and walked beside Linda without a word. She put her arm around Linda's shoulders. The two women walked the thirty feet back to the fellowship hall together, and Grace stayed with her the whole way.

Frank noticed.

• • •

By four o'clock, the room was still uncomfortably warm. Ray still hadn't apologized to Brian, and Brian hadn't brought it up. Pat and Marjorie had slipped back into quietly disliking each other. Ellen kept crying off and on. The kids asked Joanne three times when they could go home, and each time, Joanne forced a smile that took more out of her than she could spare.

Frank knew he had to do something. He told himself that a well-crafted sermon might help calm the congregation. For hours, as the tension grew, Frank thought about what to say. He had been doing this for twenty years. He stepped onto the low platform at the end of the fellowship hall, the same one used for Christmas skits. He cleared his throat, and the congregation looked up.

He began with Job.

He explained that when Job's three friends visited him during his suffering, they sat with him in silence for seven days and nights because they saw how deep his grief was. He said this was where good pastoral care begins: being willing to sit quietly with someone in pain.

Next, he spoke about Romans 8. Paul wrote that nothing could separate believers from God's love—not height, not depth, not rulers, not powers. Whatever they were facing now, it wasn't stronger than the love that had always held them, even before they came into this room.

He mentioned Bonhoeffer writing letters to his fiancée from Tegel prison. He pointed out that the church had faced dark times before, and had gotten through them by staying together. He reminded everyone that they were the communion of saints, and that wherever they were, they were not alone.

It was a solid mini-sermon. His sentences were well put together, and the transitions worked. He took his time, giving each point just enough attention. On a Sunday morning after a tough week, with the organ playing softly in the sanctuary, it might have moved the congregation.

But here, it didn't.

Grace quietly said amen during the part about Romans 8. Ray nodded when Bonhoeffer was mentioned. A few people listened politely. Linda kept her eyes on the piano bench. Marjorie kept knitting. Joanne held her younger son's hand but didn't look at Frank. Megan watched from her corner, her face blank.

Frank finished. Since no one else did, he said amen himself and stepped down from the platform.

Within two minutes, Pat and Marjorie were arguing again, though more quietly. Ray was back at the map. Joanne was back with the boys. The room looked just as it had before Frank spoke.

Standing at the edge of the platform, Frank realized his words hadn't made a difference. He had given a sermon to people who hadn't wanted one. He walked over and leaned in the kitchen doorway.

• • •

Megan stood up from her folding chair and walked across the room. She avoided looking at Frank as she passed. When she reached him, she stood next to him, both of them facing out into the room.

"Pastor Frank."

She almost never called him that.

"Yeah."

"Can I tell you something?"

"Sure."

"You talk about people. From the pulpit. You talk about them all the time. The lost. The hurting. The neighbor. You have a really good vocabulary for it." She paused. Her tone was calm, the same one she used when she was pointing out something that wasn't quite right. "But...You don't help them. Not really. You talk about them and then you go to your office."

Frank opened his mouth.

"Pastor...I'm – I'm not done." Megan's words were firm yet respectful.

"I've been at the booth three years. I have watched you walk past Linda in the foyer for three years. I have watched you flag emails from people who needed you and not respond to them. Remember Marcus? I watched you give Marcus Leite a thirty-minute lecture in your office and not follow up with a call as far as I know. I watched, Pastor. The booth is the best seat in the house for watching."

She took a small breath.

"They don't need a sermon right now. They need somebody to just be with them. You're really, really good at giving sermons. The other thing is the part you don't do..." Her voice dropped. "...Sorry."

She didn't mean for her words to come across as harsh or uncaring. She was usually straightforward, like the time she told him his office felt warm one Wednesday afternoon. It was just something she noticed, and she'd thought about it for three years before finally saying it.

Frank opened his mouth again. For thirty years, he had defended his ministry and his sermons to critics. The usual response was already forming in his mind, something gentle and thoughtful that would acknowledge her point and then put it in a broader theological context.

The standard response arrived at his mouth quickly and then Frank stopped.

Instead, what he felt, plain and sudden, was the realization that Megan was right.

He said, almost unintelligibly, "I don't know how to do that."

Megan nodded once and then she walked back to her corner.

Frank stood in the kitchen doorway. He kept thinking about the name Marcus Leite, unable to get it out of his mind.

His hand moved into his pocket involuntarily. The stone was hot.

• • •

By five, everyone in the room was worn out. Ray had dozed off sitting at the map table, his arms stretched out on the paper and his head resting on them. Joanne had settled the boys on a pile of coats by the far wall. Eli was asleep with his mouth open, while his older brother only pretended to be. Tom made himself another peanut butter sandwich. The Youngs were reading something together on Brian's phone. Marjorie kept knitting. Paul had switched from playing solitaire to laying out cards for gin rummy, but he never started the game.

Linda sat at the piano, but she hadn't played. She turned sideways on the bench, away from the keys. Grace was sitting beside her.

Sometime in the last hour, Grace left her table, crossed the room, and sat next to Linda on the piano bench without saying a word. She wasn't reading or praying out loud. She was simply present. Linda's hand rested in Grace's, and Grace traced slow, gentle circles on the back of Linda's hand with her thumb.

From the doorway of the fellowship hall, Frank watched the two women on the bench.

For the first time since coming home from Salem, he remembered the woman on the park bench. She wore a grey fleece pullover, her phone screen glowing against her leg. Her shoulders had drawn in, as if she wanted to disappear. Frank could picture her face clearly, since he always remembered details.

But he didn't know her name because he never asked.

The October light faded through the fellowship hall windows as evening came. Across Route 28A, the pitch pine trees lost their color in the dusk. Outside, night was falling as it always did at the end of a day on Cape Cod. Inside, the congregation settled in around him. Frank had not moved from the doorway.

He was starting to understand.

Chapter 7

The Rooms

Frank stood in the doorway, his hand resting on the stone in his jacket pocket, and he felt something he couldn't quite name. He thought of the stone, the woman on the park bench, the endless hallway, and the food pantry email he had ignored. Dave Fernandes had been part of the congregation for two years, but Frank only learned his name because of a window. For six years, Marcus Leite, whom Megan had just mentioned, lingered in the back of Frank's mind. The realization came quietly. There was a pattern here, but Frank hadn't noticed it until now.

He did not yet have a theology for what he was seeing. It had a distinct form. That form was only beginning to take shape in Frank's mind.

He looked across the fellowship hall at Megan. She sat in her corner, focused on her phone, scrolling between her camera roll and the bulletin map she had been marking up for hours. Her stillness felt different now. Frank noticed the change the way he noticed a shift in the weather, not directly, but by how he adjusted to it.

She was creating something.

He crossed the room.

He had never done that before, not in twenty years at this church. Frank had spent those years greeting people at the door and speaking from the pulpit, but he wasn't used to walking across a room to someone without a reason. Still, he did it now. He walked across the fellowship hall and stopped by her chair.

"Megan."

She looked up.

"Have you been working on something?"

"Yeah."

She paused and studied his face. Frank felt as if she was reading him, like a technician checking a waveform for problems.

"Yeah," she said again. "I think I have a pattern of some kind. ya know."

"Can you show me?"

"I think I should show everyone."

"Yeah. Sounds good."

• • •

She didn't call a meeting. She walked to the center table, spread out the bulletin map beside the ones she'd drawn over the past day, and said loudly, "Hey, I want to show you guys something."

Everyone gathered. Ray came over from where he'd been dozing. Tom set down his peanut butter sandwich. The Youngs left their table. The Bentos and the Monteiros joined in. Dave came over. Joanne stayed near the boys but listened in. Linda stayed on the piano bench but turned to face the room, with Grace beside her.

Megan didn't wait for everyone to quiet down. She set her phone on the table and opened the grid on her photo app.

"Okay. Every time someone has gone into the strange parts of the building since Wednesday night, I've taken pictures. I've also marked the map whenever someone opened a door. The photos are time-stamped, and I have the metadata. If you compare where and when things happened with who was walking where, you start to see a pattern."

She turned on her phone's flashlight and traced a line across the map. Frank watched her hand move. The map was covered with notes—small arrows, penciled times, and circles marking locked doors.

"Every time somebody goes in, the building changes. The hallways get longer in the direction the person is walking. New branches open up where they go, and new rooms appear at the ends of the corridors they choose."

"So it's not just changing at random?" Ray asked.

"It's kind of directing us. It moves toward us, not away. At first, I thought it wanted to trap us, but now I think it's trying to lead us somewhere specific."

It went quiet.

Ray broke the silence. "Somewhere specific—what do you mean?"

"I have no idea. But the rooms matter—the ones we haven't opened. The locked one Marjorie tried, and the others at the ends of hallways where we stopped. Those rooms are important. Somehow, they matter."

• • •

Tom Hall said, "I'll go."

The room seemed to shift. Tom sat in his hoodie, in his usual chair, speaking in that voice he used when he hadn't really made up his mind yet.

"I'm not — listen. I went and drew the X last night and the hallway moved. So I know. I know it does that. But Megan says the rooms matter. I've just been sitting here. I'd rather do something useful than keep doing nothing."

"Tom." Ray spoke, not sure if this was a good idea.

"Just one. Pair me with somebody. I'll go to the closest one."

Ray looked at the map, then at Tom, and finally at Frank.

"Take the front-door hallway," Ray said. "Not the long one. The first hallway. Not deep. Don't open a door without coming back to tell us first."

"I'll go with him," Frank said.

Tom looked at Frank.

"You don't have to."

"I know. I want to."

He didn't, not really, but he wanted to be the kind of pastor who did. Tonight, all he could do was offer. Frank had also been waiting since five, looking for a reason to walk through one of those doors he kept avoiding, since he was running out of excuses not to.

Megan said, "Take the connector. Not the front door. The hallway off the connector is the one that was lengthening. I think that one will give you the closest room."

Tom stood up. Then Frank. They walked to the connector door. Frank's hand was in his pocket. The stone was hot.

• • •

Tom went first. He pushed the door open and stepped into the hallway that had not been there forty-eight hours ago, and Frank stepped after him, and Megan watched them go from the doorway with her phone in her hand.

The hallway looked the same as always, with pine baseboards, beige walls, and fluorescent lights above. They walked ten steps, then twenty, then thirty. The hallway did not stretch ahead of them because it did not have to; it already had everything it needed. After about forty steps, a door appeared on the right. This door was not part of the original building. The wall had created it. Made of pine, it was narrower than the other church doors and had an iron knob.

Tom stared at the door, then glanced back at Frank, who stood three feet behind him.

"We promised Ray we'd come back."

"Yeah."

"Yeah, but the door's right here, Frank."

"Yeah."

Tom put his hand on the knob.

He turned it.

The door opened into a small room, probably about ten by eight feet. The floor was bare wood, and a single bulb hung from a cord. The walls were painted beige over what looked like old horsehair plaster, the kind Frank had only seen in renovated colonial houses on the upper Cape, the kind you could date if you knew what to look for. The room felt cold. It was much colder than the rest of the labyrinth, maybe ten degrees lower.

In the corner, against the far wall, sat a kid.

He looked about seventeen. He was skinny, curled up with his knees to his chest, his face mostly hidden by his arms. He was shaking, not because of the cold, but for another reason. Frank had been a pastor long enough to recognize withdrawal.

The kid looked up. His eyes found Tom first.

"Mister, you found me," he said. His voice was a thin thread. "Oh my God. You found me."

Tom didn't move. He stopped at the threshold, his hands going in and out of his pockets, but he didn't step inside.

Frank put his hand on Tom's back. He did not push. He just rested it there for a second.

"Tom. Go in."

Tom looked at him. Something was off in his face. The grin and casual swagger were gone. His mouth hung slightly open.

"Pastor."

"Yeah."

"That kid was at the youth pizza night. Three weeks ago, I think… I think he came with somebody, or — I don't —"

"Go in, Tom. I'll wait here."

• • •

Tom stepped inside, moving slowly. He sat on the floor a few feet from the kid, close enough to share the space but not so close as to make him uncomfortable. Resting his hands on his knees, he waited.

The kid's eyes filled with tears.

"I came in three weeks ago. To the youth thing. You were there. I'd been clean for six months, but I relapsed the night before. I don't really know why I came in. I just needed help. I talked to you after."

Tom tried to remember. His face changed as he searched for the memory, piecing it together from fragments that didn't have a clear label.

"You gave me a paper. With a phone number on it. The county clinic."

"Yeah. I think I remember." Tom spoke quietly. He wasn't sure. He remembered Saturday pizza nights and handing out some clinic pamphlets by the door, but he couldn't place this kid's face in any of those memories. Not being able to remember felt worse than remembering. "What's your name?"

"Jaylen."

"How long have you been here, Jaylen."

"I don't know." He pressed his forehead to his knees. "Three days. Maybe. My phone died."

Three days. Tom couldn't get it out of his head. The congregation had only been in the building for a day and a half, but this kid had already been here longer than anyone. He'd come here from a different part of his life.

"I didn't call the number." Jaylen spoke quietly, looking down at his knees. "I went home. I got high."

Tom didn't say anything right away. He sat on the floor, hands on his knees, and let the silence linger.

He pulled off his hoodie, revealing a long-sleeved T-shirt underneath. Then he slid the hoodie across the floor to Jaylen, who stared at it.

"You're shaking," Tom said. "It's cold in here. Put it on."

Jaylen put it on over his own shirt. His hands shook too much to zip it, so he gave up and pulled the hood over his head. The church logo on the front, which Tom had designed and ordered too many of, rested on his chest.

Jaylen looked pale and weak. "I'm going to come back," Tom said. "Okay? I'm going to tell the others what's happening, and I'm going to come back with water. And I'm going to sit in this doorway until you tell me to leave. All right?"

Jaylen did not answer. Tom took it as a yes.

• • •

Tom came back to the fellowship hall with Frank about twenty minutes after he left. His face looked different. He did not seem scared, but there was a new hardness in his expression.

"Red, there's a kid in there. Jaylen."

Ray said, "In the strange part of the building."

"He's in a room. A real kid. He's going through withdrawal. He says he's been there for three days. He came to a youth event three weeks ago, and we gave him a pamphlet."

Grace closed her eyes. Marjorie set down her knitting. The room grew quiet in a way it hadn't before, not even during Frank's talk that afternoon.

Ray asked, "What did you do?"

"I sat in the doorway. I told him I'd come back. I gave him my hoodie because the room was cold."

Tom looked back with a steadiness Frank hadn't seen in him before.

"He's real, Frank. You saw him too, right? He's a real person. He's here in this building right now."

Megan was at the map. She didn't look up while Tom spoke. She marked a small dot at the edge of the fellowship hall connector and drew a short arrow labeled J. She understood before Tom finished.

• • •

Ray said what everyone was thinking.

"If there's one, there could be more."

Megan nodded. She had been waiting for somebody to say it.

Ray paired everyone up just like he had on Wednesday night, but the room felt heavier now. He teamed up with Paul Bento. The Youngs went together. Dave was with one of the Monteiros. Frank was with Megan. Joanne stayed with the boys, and Linda stayed with Grace.

The groups entered a few minutes apart, making sure the hallways stayed clear for Megan's instructions. The building made it possible.

Ray and Paul were the first to return, but they showed up forty minutes after they were supposed to be back in twenty.

Ray and Paul walked down the corridor off the chapel branch. Paul counted three hundred and twenty paces before they reached a door made of pine with an iron knob. They both heard the latch click open as Paul turned it.

The room was small and cold. There was a cot, a duffel bag, and a man sleeping with his face to the wall. His work boots were lined up neatly at the foot of the cot, and his beard was turning grey.

Ray recognized him by his boots first, the kind a man without a place to sleep might wear. Then he saw the duffel bag, and finally the back of his head with that short gray hair Ray had seen driving past the Mashpee rotary for three years.

The man's name came up from somewhere Ray had not used in a while. "Darnell."

Ray said it under his breath, more to himself than to the room. The man on the cot did not stir.

Paul reached for the doorframe behind him to steady himself. The door closed under his hand, moving smoothly as if on a strong spring. By the time he let go, the latch had already clicked into place. He tried the knob. It turned, but the door stayed shut.

"Red," Paul said quietly.

The room was small. Ten feet by eight. One bare bulb. The man on the cot, asleep.

"Red, it's not opening."

"Lock?"

"There's no lock on this door, Red. It just isn't opening."

Ray didn't panic. He had spent forty years on job sites where doors sometimes locked behind you because of wind, a wedge, a kid, or a hinge. He knew how to handle that, but he had no words for what happened next.

The man on the cot rolled over.

He looked at Ray.

He did not look surprised or afraid. He looked like someone who had been waiting a long time for a certain person to walk through that door, and was now deciding if Ray was the one he had been waiting for.

He sat up. The cot creaked.

"Ray Pacheco."

Ray went very still.

"Yeah."

"From the church on 28A."

"Yeah."

Darnell was quiet for a long moment. He did not have to say anything; the silence said enough. Paul, behind Ray, let go of the knob and dropped his hand to his side. He stayed quiet too, just as he had learned on a boat in rough weather for thirty-two years, knowing when to speak and when to keep silent.

Ray stayed silent for what felt like forever, though it was only a few seconds. "I gave you twenty bucks. Three years ago. November. You were standing at the rotary in a green Carhartt jacket with the right pocket torn."

"Yeah."

"I asked your name. You told me... I forgot it. I drove home and I forgot it before I got to the bridge."

"Yeah."

"I'm sorry."

"I know."

Darnell glanced at the door, then at Paul, and finally back at Ray.

"You can leave in a minute. The door will let you out. Try not to worry about it."

Ray didn't know how Darnell could tell. He didn't ask. After forty years on job sites, Ray knew when to keep quiet, and this was one of those times, especially in a room that wasn't on any blueprint he recognized.

After a long pause, Darnell said, "You gonna come back?"

It wasn't really a question. It felt more like a test. Ray sensed it deeply, as if it was something he had avoided for years and now had no choice but to confront.

"Yeah," Ray said.

"All right."

"I'll come back."

"All right."

The door opened quietly. Paul noticed and stepped back. The corridor was still there, just like before. The room stayed cold, Darnell did not move, and the door stayed open.

Ray took his time. He glanced at Darnell on the cot for a moment. Then he stepped into the corridor, Paul following behind, and together they walked the three hundred and twenty paces back to the connector door without speaking.

The door behind them stayed open as they left. Ray did not look back because he already knew it was open. The building had already said what it needed to say.

• • •

Ray came back into the fellowship hall looking as pale as wax. He sat at the map table, placed his hand flat on it, and avoided looking at anyone for a long moment.

Then he spoke, his words plain and almost like a confession: "His name is Darnell. He's a man I've been driving past at the Mashpee rotary for three years. I gave him twenty bucks once. I went home and forgot his name before I got to the bridge. I just told him I'd come back."

Paul stayed quiet. He didn't need to say anything. Ray had already said it.

The Youngs returned next.

They weren't alone.

A woman in her early forties stood in the doorway behind Ellen, where the hall led to the labyrinth. She stayed at the threshold, not coming in. She wore a light brown cardigan and jeans, with only socks on her feet, as if she had been waiting somewhere for a long time. Her hands were empty, and her face was dry.

She stayed on the labyrinth side of the doorway, resting one hand on the door frame, and looked at everyone in the fellowship hall. Everyone looked back at her. The room fell silent, the kind of quiet that happens when something people have tried to ignore finally appears.

Ellen, still in the doorway with her, said, quietly: "Her name is Sarah."

Sarah stayed silent. She held the jamb and looked at the table, where the remains of the potluck sat—the picked-over ziti, the untouched Jell-O mold, the crumbled cookies. She glanced at Linda at the piano, and Linda met her gaze. Sarah looked at Linda longer than she looked at anything else. Then she looked at the empty folding chairs in the back row, the ones a woman in a light brown cardigan would have sat in about eight months ago.

Finally, Sarah spoke in a flat, expressionless voice: "It's not as big as I remembered."

"Sarah. Do you want to come in?" Ellen asked softly.

Sarah looked at Ellen, unsure if she could trust her with a thought she'd held onto for a long time. She glanced back into the fellowship hall, then at the back row of chairs again, and finally at Linda at the piano.

"Not yet."

She let go of the jamb, turned, and walked back into the labyrinth in her socks. The corridor seemed to stretch ahead of her. Brian started to follow, but Ellen placed her hand on his arm.

"She'll be in her room. She wants to be there. We can go back."

Ellen turned to face the fellowship hall. She hadn't cried in the doorway, but now tears came quietly, just as they had throughout the day. This time, though, something about it felt different. She walked over to the nearest folding chair and sat down hard.

"I don't remember her last name," Ellen said, her eyes lowered. "She came to the Sunday service eight months ago and sat in the back row. She left before the sermon finished. I was there. Brian was there. We saw her, sitting alone in a light brown cardigan, but we didn't go over. She's running from her husband. She's been running for a year. She needed a quiet place to sit and think, so she came to our church. In the hour she was here, nobody spoke to her."

Brian sat next to Ellen and put his arm around her. He stayed silent.

Dave and Pat Monteiro were the third to return. They had found a room with just one armchair. An older man, maybe seventy, sat there wearing a VFW cap, his hands resting very still in his lap. He didn't answer their questions. His eyes were open, but he wasn't looking at them. Pat recognized the cap and thought the man might have come to a Christmas Eve service a year or two ago, though he wasn't sure. When they finally got his name, it was Walter. He was a Vietnam veteran and, by his sense of time, he had been in the building for weeks.

Dave and Pat hadn't stayed. Standing in the hallway, they agreed Walter probably didn't want company, and leaving him alone for an hour seemed respectful. They knew they were probably wrong, so they came back to ask for advice.

Frank and Megan were the fourth to go.

They walked down a corridor that seemed to stretch on for about 1500 feet. Frank kept his hand in his jacket pocket the entire way. The stone inside felt warm against his palm.

They came to a door.

It was the only door at the end of the corridor, made of pine. The wood looked older than any pine in the original church, its grain worn as if it had been closed for a hundred years.

Frank stopped at the threshold. He did not touch the knob.

Megan waited quietly, patient and saying nothing.

He stayed there a long time.

Frank said, finally, "I'm not ready."

Megan nodded.

They walked back to the fellowship hall.

• • •

They gave their report. Frank just said that he and Megan had reached a door but he hadn't opened it. Megan didn't say anything to add or correct him. Ray took their report and didn't ask any questions.

After they finished reporting, Megan turned back to the map. She tapped the notes she had made while everyone was out. Jaylen. Darnell. Sarah. Walter. Four names, four rooms, four small dots on a bulletin that, just two days ago, had been a church announcement for a Wednesday potluck.

"The building isn't trapping us by chance," she said. "It's matching us with certain people. It wants us to sit with them. I don't think it will let us leave until we do."

No one spoke for a long time.

Then Ray spoke. "Are you saying the building is judging us?"

"I don't know what to call it. But it seems clear to me that the building is trying to match us with someone or some thing… I don't know. I think what is clear is that every person is matched to a stranger. Jaylen was Tom's. Darnell was yours. Sarah was the Youngs'. Walter was someone's."

"How do we know who we're matched with?"

"The building pushes you toward them. You felt it. Right?"

Ray didn't argue. He had felt it too.

Grace, standing by the piano with her hand still in Linda's: "Is this the Lord, Megan?"

Megan paused. She was seventeen and had grown up with parents who weren't religious. She didn't want to be the one to answer that question.

"I don't know, Grace. I don't know if the Lord is behind this or if it's something else. But whatever it is, it knows exactly what we did and didn't do."

Grace accepted the answer and didn't ask anything else.

Frank hung at the edge of the group with his hand on the stone. The stone felt extremely hot. He remembered the woman on the park bench in Salem— the grey fleece pullover, the phone screen glowing against her leg, and the way her shoulders had pulled in.

He had walked right past her.

He knew he would have to open the door he hadn't opened tonight. Not now, but soon. The building wasn't going to let him leave it closed.

• • •

The congregation didn't decide together what to do next. Instead, people started to act on their own.

Brian and Ellen Young took two folding chairs from the stack by the wall and a blanket from the donation bin under the coat rack, then went back for Sarah. They didn't know what they would say to her, but they went anyway.

Ray didn't return to Darnell. He sat at the map with his hand on it, avoiding everyone's eyes. He said quietly, "I need a minute." No one argued.

Tom stood up, took a bottle of water from the food table, and left. He didn't say where he was going. He didn't need to.

Dave and Pat Monteiro talked quietly about Walter for a while. They decided to wait another hour before checking on him again.

Standing at the edge of the fellowship hall, Frank watched his congregation change since the potluck began. Brian carried a folding chair into what looked like an impossible situation. Tom walked back through a door with a water bottle. Ray faced his own failure, which was the first honest thing he had done in twenty-two years of keeping the church's books perfectly.

Megan stood at the map, adding the new rooms to her notes in small, neat letters. Jaylen. Darnell. Sarah. Walter. Four names. Four rooms. Four people the church missed when it had the chance.

Across the room, Grace still sat on the piano bench with Linda. She hadn't moved since this afternoon.

Frank turned away from the door at the end of the long hallway.

He walked toward the piano.

Chapter 8

Staying

Frank walked over to the piano. He didn't sit on the bench because there wasn't space for him, and he wasn't someone who liked to share benches. Instead, he grabbed a folding chair from a nearby table and placed it a few feet from Grace and Linda. Then he sat down.

He did not say anything.

He tried to do what Grace did so well, but he didn't know how. He had no words, no plan, and no method. Right now, all he had was a folding chair and the choice to stay.

Grace didn't look at him, but the corner of her mouth shifted. It was like a nod, just without moving her head.

Linda's hand was still in Grace's. Linda's eyes were on the keys she was not playing.

Frank stayed silent for a long time. In the past, he always filled uncertainty with words. Now, he tried to let the silence be, but it was hard for him. He didn't know what to do with his hands.

On the other side of the fellowship hall, Megan set herself up at the map table. She had Ray's tape measure, a pencil, and a small plastic ruler from the children's craft box in the kitchen. Her bulletin map was spread out next to the roof-project blueprint Frank had brought from his office earlier. Her phone was open to the photo grid.

She was creating a system. It was her way of fixing things.

On the first night, Wednesday, Megan had panicked. She didn't like to admit it, but it was true. When the corridors started to stretch, she grabbed a bulletin and tried to draw what she saw, but her hand shook too much to make a straight line. She drew two corridors in the wrong order. She labeled the chapel branch as east, even though it was clearly west, and didn't notice the mistake for forty minutes. By eleven-thirty, she put her head down on the table with the bulletin underneath. Frank hadn't seen her do it. No one had. After midnight, she crumpled the bulletin into the kitchen trash, went to the bathroom, washed her face, and stood at the sink, telling herself quietly to stop being seventeen.

On Thursday morning, she began again. The fear had left her hands and settled somewhere quieter behind her ribs. Now, with a tape measure and a small plastic ruler from the kids' craft box, she was making her second attempt.

She had already measured the hallway to Jaylen's room before Tom left with the water bottle about twenty minutes earlier. She wrote the number of paces on the bulletin board in small, careful pencil. She hadn't told anyone what she was doing. She wanted her data to be clean.

• • •

Ray spent an hour at the map table with his hand flat on the paper before he stood up. He didn't say anything. He walked across the fellowship hall, through the connector door, and into the strange hallway.

The hallway stretched out in front of him, the way everyone had gotten used to. He didn't resist. He let the building lead him to the room it had chosen for him. He walked for what felt like ten or fifteen minutes, not keeping track.

He reached the door and opened it.

Darnell was still on the cot, but now he was awake. He sat up as Ray entered.

Ray did what he always did. He was a builder, someone who solved problems. Even after four hours at the map table, taking in what the door had told him, he couldn't help but come into the room and start cataloguing: the cot, the duffel bag, the work boots lined up neatly at the foot. His cataloguing always turned into offers.

"All right. I came back, like I said. We've got coffee in the other room. There's still food from the potluck—soup, sandwiches. I can get you some. I can't get you out of the building tonight. Something's wrong with the building, you know that. But we've got food and a place out of this cold room and—"

Darnell let him talk. He had been through this conversation before. He had heard men like this offer help a thousand times, and he knew most of the help ended as soon as the person offering it felt he had done his part.

When Ray finished, Darnell spoke quietly. "Ray." He let out a tired breath. "I don't want soup."

Ray stopped.

"I want you to look at me."

Ray looked at him.

"Not — not at what I need. At me."

Ray tried. He really was trying, but he wasn't good at it. He had spent forty years framing houses and twenty-two years counting the offering, but looking at another person—seeing who they really were—was something he had never been asked to do.

Then he did something he hadn't done in front of anyone since his father died in 1982. He didn't realize it was coming. He eased himself down to the floor, not trusting his knees. The floor was bare pine. Ray Pacheco never sat on the floor, but today he did. His eyes filled with tears. He let them be.

"My old man," Ray said. He hadn't planned to say it, but the room brought it out. "My old man was Manuel Pacheco. He ran a fishing boat out of New Bedford. He drowned in '82. I was twenty-eight. He was sixty-one. He went out alone in November in a boat he should have replaced two years earlier. The wind came up off Buzzards Bay, the boat flipped, and they found him on the third day."

He stopped. Darnell stayed quiet. Darnell hadn't asked, and somehow that made it easier for Ray to speak.

I didn't go to his funeral. We argued. For twenty years, we argued before he drowned, and those words stayed with me when he died. I told my mother I was working in Hyannis, sent flowers, and didn't go. My older sister hasn't spoken to me since. She lives in Fall River. Forty years, Darnell. Forty years, and missing that funeral has cost me everything I haven't let myself feel about my father.

He pressed his hand against his eye.

"I've kept the church's books for twenty-two years. I once gave a homeless man at the rotary a twenty-dollar bill, then went home and forgot his name. Those two things are really the same. I'm Manuel Pacheco's son. I cut myself off from my father, and I've been cutting myself off from every man who's needed me since."

He kept going.

"The worst part is this. I have a pickup with a bench seat, plenty of room. I've driven past you in February, wind coming off the sound, my heater and radio on, and not once in three years did I slow down to ask if you needed a ride."

Darnell let him finish. Then, moving slowly with stiff joints, Darnell lowered himself to the floor across the room. They sat against opposite walls in a small room in a building that shouldn't exist, looking at each other.

Darnell said, "My name is Darnell Foster."

"Ray Pacheco."

"I know. Somebody said your name when I walked into the service two years ago. I was looking for a bathroom. I came in the side door. I was going to leave before anybody saw me. Somebody said Ray and I looked over and you were counting money on a table in the back."

Ray closed his eyes.

They sat in silence for a long time. There was no need for words. Ray began to cry, his sobs nearly silent, his jaw tight and his body rigid. Darnell did not try to comfort him. He was not there to comfort Ray. He was there to be seen, and Ray was there to see him. That was what mattered.

They sat for over an hour.

• • •

After Ray left, Megan measured the hallway to Darnell's room. She paced it, counting quietly. It was one hundred and twenty-seven steps down the corridor without stopping.

At some point she could not pinpoint, the corridor became shorter. She had been looking at her phone when it happened. She walked to the fellowship hall connector door, opened it a little, and paced the hallway again.

Ninety-four paces.

She wrote the number on her bulletin next to Darnell's dot. She wrote the time. She waited three hundred seconds, counting them in her head, and paced it a third time.

Ninety-four.

She turned to the room.

"The hallway to Ray's room has gotten shorter."

Frank, across the room, looked up.

Linda, on the bench, did not look up.

Grace, beside her, did.

• • •

Tom returned to Jaylen's hallway with water and a Pop-Tart. He also brought a second bottle of water for himself, unsure how long he would be sitting on the floor, but he had made up his mind to stay.

Jaylen was awake. He had finished half the water, but the Pop-Tart still sat unopened beside him.

"My folks live in Mashpee," Jaylen said, staring at the floor. "They kicked me out in June. My mom did. She found me in the bathroom with a needle and told me I was done. By dinner, my suitcases were on the porch. Some nights I stay with my cousin Andre in Bourne, or with my buddy Steve if he has a couch. The rest of the time, I'm at the camp on Route 28 near Hyannis."

Tom said, "The camp."

"The encampment. You drive by it—the one in the woods. There are tents, tarps, about fifteen of us."

Tom had driven past it many times. He had never stopped.

"You run the Tuesday-night thing, right? I came in three weeks ago because it was Saturday night, the camp was soaked, and I'd been clean for six months but was about to relapse. I'd walked past your church a hundred times. I saw the sign for the Saturday-night pizza thing. So I went in. I saw the kids— fourteen, fifteen years old, my brother's age. I felt stupid and sat in the back. Eventually, you came over."

Tom waited without interrupting. He didn't say he remembered, because he didn't.

"I told you I needed help. I used those exact words. I said I need help. You said, yeah, of course, what kind. I told you I'd been clean but was about to use again and needed to talk to someone who understood. You reached into your back pocket and pulled out a little card. You said it was the county clinic, a twenty-four-hour line, and they were great—they helped a guy you knew last year. You told me to call the number, said you'd pray for me, patted my shoulder, and went back to the kids."

Jaylen swallowed. His Adam's apple moved beneath his skin.

"I went back to the camp. It was raining still. I sat in a wet tent. I called the number. They said they had a five-day wait list and I should call back in the morning to see if there was an opening. I hung up. I used. Three weeks straight since then."

Tom did not say anything for a while.

When he finally spoke, his voice sounded flat in a way Frank, listening from the end of the hallway, had never heard before.

"Jaylen. I am so sorry."

"It's okay."

"It's not okay."

"It's okay, Pastor."

Tom didn't remember Jaylen. He'd been sitting across from the kid for forty minutes tonight, but the face wasn't familiar. He couldn't recall a desperate teenager coming to him after a Saturday pizza night.

"Jaylen. I handed you that pamphlet?"

"Yeah."

"I don't remember you. I have been sitting here looking at you and trying to remember you and I don't."

"I know."

"My job is teenagers and I do not remember the one teenager who came to me asking for help."

Jaylen didn't have an answer. He didn't try to comfort Tom or say it's okay again.

Tom rested his forehead on his knees. He didn't cry now. He would cry later. For now, he just took it in.

After a long minute, he lifted his head. "Okay. I'm going to sit here, Jaylen. I'll stay as long as you let me. And tomorrow, if we get out of here, I'll drive you to a detox clinic myself. No pamphlet. I'll walk you through the door. And I'll remember your name."

Jaylen nodded. He didn't smile. There was no redemption in it, but his shoulders dropped just a little.

• • •

Megan paced the hallway to Jaylen's branching. It was fifty-two steps from the connector door to where Tom had marked an X last night. She wrote down the number and compared it to yesterday's measurement, which had been seventy-eight.

She turned to the room.

"Tom's hallway too."

Ray, back from Darnell's room, face still wet, sitting at the map: "How much?"

"Twenty-six paces."

Ray nodded slowly.

• • •

Linda stood up from the piano bench around midnight.

Grace held onto Linda's hand for a moment longer. She looked at Linda, who nodded. Then Grace let go. Linda crossed the fellowship hall, went through the connector door, and entered the unfamiliar part of the building.

The hallway stretched out in front of her, but she didn't question it. She walked for a long time. The corridor never seemed to get shorter; it just kept going. Eventually, she reached a door. It wasn't the one Brian and Ellen had described. This was a different door in a different hallway, and Linda somehow knew the building had made a separate entrance just for her.

She opened it.

Sarah sat in the small office, her hands wrapped around a cup of tea. When Linda entered, Sarah looked up. Linda was forty-five, and Sarah was forty-three. They recognized each other in the way women do when they've spent their lives performing for others.

Linda did what she always did. She walked in, sat in the empty chair across from Sarah, and took her hand. Then she said:

"Can we pray?"

Sarah flinched at the question.

It was just a small flinch, barely a millimeter of withdrawal. But Linda had played piano at thousands of Sunday services, and her skill was noticing the smallest reactions in a room. She saw it.

"I'm sorry," Sara said. "I — no. Yes. You can pray. I just — I haven't —"

Linda let go of her hand but stayed seated. She waited.

Sarah tried again. "My husband is a deacon."

There was a pause.

"...was a deacon. At the Methodist church in Orleans. He prays over our dinner every night. He also broke my arm in August. I haven't been able to — when I hear the word husband I just —"

Linda listened quietly, absorbing everything. She and Mike had been married for nineteen years, but for nearly two years, they hadn't spent time alone together outside the bedroom they no longer shared. Mike wasn't violent, and he wasn't a deacon. To anyone looking in, he seemed like a good husband. Still, their marriage had felt hollow since their son left for college four years ago, and Linda tried to fill that emptiness with Sunday worship. Every Tuesday afternoon, while Mike played golf and the house was silent, Linda cried. She had never shared any of this with anyone before.

Now, she finally spoke the words. She sat in a place that might not even be real, across from a woman whose husband prayed before dinner and had once broken her arm.

"I don't... I don't pray when I'm at the piano. I know people think I do. I look like I do. I close my eyes. I feel the music. I am not praying, Sarah. I'm hiding. I have been hiding in worship for four years because my marriage is dead and I cant face it. My husband isn't dangerous. He's just gone. I'm alone, and I've been pretending to be a woman in love with the Lord because it was easier than being a woman whose husband won't look at her."

She said it all in one breath. She didn't cry. She had spent four years crying in private. The only place she refused to cry was the place where she finally allowed herself to be honest.

Sarah reached across the table. She took Linda's hand, and she turned it palm up, and she put her own hand in it.

The building around them was completely quiet. Linda noticed the silence for a moment, then let it fade into the background. It wasn't the silence of an empty room. It was the silence of two women who had stopped pretending for anyone, even themselves or each other.

They sat across the table from each other for a long time with their hands joined, and when Linda finally spoke again she said, "What do you need?"

Sarah said, "Someone to sit with me until I figure out what to do next."

"Okay?"

• • •

Megan paced the hallway to Sarah's door.

She wrote the number. She compared it.

She turned to the room.

"Linda's too."

Everyone in the room had been paying attention the whole time. Ray looked at her. Frank looked at her. Grace, still sitting alone on the piano bench, looked at her too.

Megan spoke, "Three rooms, three shortenings. It's real. I can measure it."

"How much shorter overall." Ray asked.

Megan glanced down at the bulletin. She had spent the last hour adding up paces.

"The whole place. I'd estimate a third."

Ray paused for a moment, then asked, "A third smaller in six hours?"

"About that. There's something else."

Megan set the pencil down.

"I've been logging time stamps on every measurement. Phone stamps, because that's what I had. A few hours ago I started catching the phone time and my wristwatch time off from each other by more than I could explain. I thought my watch had a dying battery. I checked it against the wall clock in the kitchen. The watch is fine. The watch and the phone are reading two different clocks."

Frank looked up from his folding chair.

"My watch right now says four eighteen in the morning. My phone says quarter past one."

The only sound was the random ticking of the boiler.

Megan continued, keeping her voice steady.

"I started watching both about three hours ago, according to my watch. The phone has only counted about an hour of that. The ratio is staying close to three to one. I'm not sure if that's exact. I'm just pacing hallways with a craft-store ruler. I'm just telling you what I think I've measured."

"The phone's on the cell tower," Ray said.

"Yeah, the phone's on the cell tower. The cell tower is outside the building."

"So you're saying three hours in here equals one hour out there?"

"I'm just saying the math lines up that way. I don't really understand it."

Ray paused for a long moment and ran his hand down his face.

"The potluck ended at... what, eight forty-five?"

"Eight forty-five on my watch. The phone said the same then. They started drifting apart sometime Wednesday night."

"So outside, by the cell tower, it's still maybe eleven on Wednesday night. Maybe quarter to twelve."

"Maybe a bit later. Not much."

Ray had been trying to figure out why no one outside had come for them. No spouses, no police, no family, not even a neighbor with a flashlight. Since Thursday afternoon, he'd told himself that Cape Cod Wednesday potlucks were small enough that no one would notice until late Friday at the earliest. He hadn't really believed it.

"So nobody's coming," Ray said, his voice almost flat.

"Not yet. Not for a while, if my math's right," Megan replied in nearly the same tone.

Grace, who had been listening from the piano bench, said, "It's the building."

"I think so. I think the building is keeping us here long enough to do whatever it's doing, on its own time. The outside world won't notice we're missing until maybe Thursday morning, by the cell tower. By then, we'll have lived through what feels like all of Friday in here."

The boiler kept ticking.

Frank said, "It's holding us until it thinks we're ready to leave."

Megan looked at him.

"Yeah."

She picked up a pencil and wrote a note in the margin of the bulletin, underlining it twice: Time runs slow at the curb.

• • •

The eastern windows of the fellowship hall changed from black to deep blue, then to the flat gray of dawn. It was another October morning. Ray had come back from a second visit to Darnell, this time bringing blankets. Tom was still with Jaylen. Linda was still with Sarah. Dave and Pat Monteiro had talked about going back to Walter, but they hadn't gone yet. They planned to go today. Sometime during the night, they decided that just talking about it was honest, and it was fine to need another hour.

Frank sat in his folding chair by the piano. Grace remained on the bench.

The fellowship hall was quieter than it had been since Wednesday. This was not the quiet of sleep, but the kind that comes when the real work is happening somewhere else, and everyone in the room understood that.

Megan stood by the map, her notes filled with time-stamps and distances. On another page, she kept a brief list of who was still out and their locations.

Frank still hadn't gone in. The pine door at the end of the long hallway stayed closed. He knew it. Megan knew it. Grace knew it. No one mentioned it. The strange building was now a third smaller. Four rooms had been entered. One remained untouched.

Frank stood up from his folding chair and said quietly to Grace, "I think I need to go in."

Grace looked at him for a long moment. She said, "All right, Pastor."

It was the first time she'd called him that all week.

The Diagnosis

The hallway outside the sanctuary opened a little after seven that morning. Grace went to the front door out of routine, not expecting anything. She turned the knob as she had so many times in the last day and a half. This time, it turned, the door opened, and she saw the church steps in the damp October light.

Grace did not run or gasp. She stood on the top step for a moment and looked at her Buick in the lot. She checked to make sure the car was still there, as if confirming a dream. Then she walked down the steps, along the crushed-shell drive, and onto the wet grass at the edge of the parking lot.

She knelt.

She did not pray out loud. She did not need to. After thirty-six hours of praying inside a building that had kept her in, she was now outside on the wet October grass in her navy cardigan. Her knees ached, and she prayed quietly, hands resting on her thighs.

She did not ask to go back inside. She did not ask for others to be brought out. She prayed as she always did: for names. Linda. Ray. Tom. Frank. Megan. These were strangers she had met at the map table. Darnell. Sarah. Jaylen. Walter.

A Buick she did not recognize pulled into the lot at the end of the driveway. The driver saw the open door and the woman kneeling but did not stop. Grace did not know the driver. The car turned around and left. On Cape Cod, people kept to themselves.

The second couple came out forty minutes later. Grace did not stand up or look over when they did.

Two more people left within an hour after that.

Grace remained on her knees.

• • •

By mid-morning, the fellowship hall was much less crowded. Joanne and the boys had left through the sanctuary around eight. At the threshold, Eli hesitated, looked back at his mother, and quietly asked if they were really allowed to leave. Joanne said yes. Eli took three steps onto the front walk, stopped, turned around, and looked at the building for a long moment. Then he took his mother's hand and walked with her across the parking lot to the car, not letting go the whole way.

The Bentos left at nine. Marjorie gathered her knitting without saying anything, and Paul put away the cards. The Monteiros were still inside. Pat paced near the windows, as if drawn to something he had not yet chosen. His wife stood near the kitchen doorway. Both seemed quietly pulled toward the rooms that had been waiting for them.

Tom had stayed by Jaylen's doorway since last night.

Ray had visited Darnell two more times.

Linda had come out of Sarah's room, gone back in, and come out again.

Dave Fernandes and Pat Monteiro had gone to see Walter an hour ago. The door to Walter's room closed behind them.

Frank moved from the folding chair near the piano to another chair at the map table. He sat across from Megan, hands folded on the bulletin in front of him. He was waiting until he felt ready.

Megan had added her notes to a second bulletin, then a third. She'd spent fourteen hours at the map, measuring each hallway several times. Now she used colors: blue for the original church, red for shortened hallways, green for rooms they'd entered. Walter was marked with a gray circle, but she'd just changed it to green since Dave and Pat had gone in.

She'd also written notes in the margins that Frank hadn't seen before. They were short pencil lines, each ending with a question mark. *Floorboards: pine, wide, hand-planed. Older than the foyer. Much older? Trim profile: not like ours. Pre-Victorian? Fluorescent fixtures: 1950s? Same as the ones in the boiler room.*

She was following a pattern.

She looked up as Frank sat down across from her.

"You ready?"

"No. But I think I'm about to be."

"Do you want to see what I found?"

"Most definitely."

• • •

Megan turned her bulletin-map so Frank could see the notes in the margins.

"I might be wrong about some of this, just so you know. I'm not a historian. But the building isn't all the same. The hallways closest to us, the ones that showed up first on Wednesday night, look like the rest of our church. They have the same fluorescent lights and baseboards as the foyer. Those hallways have been getting shorter the fastest." Megan tapped the red lines on the bulletin. "This section. This section. Everything within the first two hundred steps of the connector door."

Frank nodded.

"The hallways further in are different. The floorboards are wider and rougher. The trim is, I guess, fancier—curlier, with little carved details at the corners that we don't have in our part of the building. The rooms are a mix. Darnell's room felt newer than Sarah's. Jaylen's closet seemed older than both, but that's just my guess."

"You've been studying the woodwork?"

"I took photos and grabbed that book on New England church architecture from your shelf. I read it for about an hour at three this morning. I think I learned enough to see that things change the deeper you go. But I don't know enough to date anything. Can you to handle that part?"

She slid her phone across the table to him, showing a grid of photos. She'd taken close-ups of trim, wide shots of floorboard seams, and details of a baseboard he didn't recognize from any wall in his church.

Frank scrolled through the photos.

He said, "The trim you called fancier is a Victorian cornice, from the mid-1800s. The wider floorboards nearby are from the same time. I know a parishioner who restores houses from that era. The parts closer in, the ones that look like our church, are from the twentieth century. You got that right."

Megan nodded but didn't write anything down. She just watched him scroll.

"Keep going. What about further in?"

"The corridors past the strangers' rooms? Paul and Dave saw box pews in the chapel that first night. Box pews are from the eighteenth century, give or take. The horsehair plaster Paul mentioned fits that time too. I'd want to see them myself to be sure."

"And here." Megan pointed to a pencil mark at the bottom corner of the bulletin. A single line led away from the fellowship hall, longer than any other note on the page. "That's the corridor to the door you didn't open. The one we walked to yesterday. The trim at that door is the oldest thing in this building. I know that much because it doesn't look like anything else. I just can't say when it's from."

She tapped her phone. The screen showed a close-up of plain pine on the door frame, hand-tooled with no machine-cut edges. The grain was wide and uneven. Behind it was rough plaster, and the horsehair fibers showed up in the photo where her phone's flash caught them.

Frank looked at the photograph for a long time.

"Hand-planed floorboards that wide stopped being made once reliable sawmills were around. The plaster behind them, with the horsehair, was only used before the Civil War.

He paused.

"The trim profile at the door? I've seen that profile once before, in a photograph from a book I read in seminary. The photo was of the meetinghouse at Ipswich. That meetinghouse was built in 1690."

He was quiet for a moment.

"I'd want to touch it myself before I could be sure. But that's what it looks like."

Megan didn't explain the meaning of the year to Frank. She didn't need to. Four Sundays ago, she was in the sound booth when Frank preached about Cotton Mather, Nicholas Noyes, and a small black stone at the base of a ledge in Salem. She had listened, figured it out over the last six hours, and now she was letting Frank come to the realization himself.

"Megan."

"Yeah."

"You're telling me the building has layers."

"I'm telling you, the building has layers. The layers go back in time. The oldest part is the deepest, and it's the part you haven't walked into yet."

"And the oldest part is 1690s."

"That's what you just told me, wasn't it?

"Yes."

•••

Frank stayed silent for a while. When he finally spoke, his words came slowly. He was thinking aloud. For the first time in twenty years at this church, he spoke to Megan as an equal.

"The stone came from Salem. I picked it up on Proctor's Ledge, where they hanged people for being what Cotton Mather said they were. I took it home like a souvenir."

Megan nodded. She had already guessed that part.

"The stone didn't bring a spirit with it. I think it was more like a seed. Three hundred years of what happened on Proctor's Ledge settled into the rock, carried along, dormant, waiting for the right place. It was a witness, too. It stood at the foot of the gallows and at Mather's horse. It heard everything. When I brought it here, it found soil. The same sin that grew in Salem was already here. The stone didn't plant it. The stone recognized it."

"What was already here?"

"The same thing that was in Salem. It's not a witch or a demon or a ghost. It's a kind of rot that grows in places that profess to follow Jesus and do not live like it. It's not the sin of the women they hanged. It's the sin of the judges. The sin of the ministers on horseback who watched the executions and quoted Scripture at the crowd."

He built his thoughts the way he built a sermon, but this was a sermon he had never given before. It was one he had avoided his whole adult life. Now, he was preaching to himself.

Frank thought through the events, then suddenly said as if reminding himself, "1692. Salem. Ministers hanging their neighbors while quoting the Bible. They had certainty without mercy...the Scriptures without application. That was the first American version of it."

"1740s. The Great Awakening. Genuine revival. Jonathan Edwards at Enfield. It was real. But it burned out inside of a decade in most places, and what replaced the revival was the form of revival without the substance. Tents without fruit."

"1800s. Slavery, and the sermons that justified it. Pastors who owned people and still preached on Sundays. Theology in service of commerce."

"Early 1900s. Protestants fighting each other about who got to define God while the cities filled up with the poor nobody welcomed."

"Mid-1900s. Billy Graham crusades filling stadiums, and in the same decade, churches arguing about what good worship music should be while they had no passion for the lost outside the walls."

"Late 1900s. The prosperity gospel. God as a vending machine. Churches the size of stadiums with parking lots full of luxury cars and no outreach to the neighborhoods they sat in."

"2000s. Tweets and posts instead of visits. Group chats and online prayer chains instead of face-to-face fellowship and care. Talking about the lost instead of going to them."

He paused and looked at Megan.

"And now. Cape Community Church. A congregation of sixty. A pastor who studies God and does not know his parishioners' names. A bulletin that says Reaching Our Community for Christ with a prayer list that does not contain one name from outside the congregation."

Megan listened, quiet and still. She never reached for her phone, which lay face-down on the bulletin.

"It's not a spirit of a witch, Megan. It's the spirit of the judges. It's what happens when the church stops being the church and becomes an institution that talks about the church. It has been here for three hundred years. It didn't come from Salem because of the stone. It was already in this building. The stone told it we were home."

He paused and looked at the map.

"The verse Grace read on Wednesday. *They profess to know God, but they deny him by their works.* That was true of Noyes under the hanging tree. It was true of Mather on his horse. It has been true of every version of this same sickness since. It has been true of Cape Community Church for at least the twenty years I've been preaching in it… It has been true of me."

• • •

Megan took it in. She paused to think about what he had said, then asked her question.

"If that's what it is, Frank. What does it want?"

Frank thought for a moment. He remembered Grace reading Titus 1:16 at two in the morning that first night. He pictured Grace on the piano bench with Linda, Ray on the floor in Darnell's room, and Tom leaning against a doorframe in the hallway.

"I don't think it wants anything. I don't think it can want. It's more like a condition. It's a diagnosis."

"Okay. A diagnosis of what?"

"Of what we are when we stop being what we're supposed to be."

Megan waited.

"There's another verse in Titus, two chapters after the one Grace read. In Titus 2, Paul says the grace of God has appeared and teaches us. It doesn't just save us, though it does. It teaches us: training us to renounce ungodliness and worldly passions, and to live self-controlled, upright, and godly lives in the present age. He paused.

"God's grace is a classroom, Megan. It doesn't only forgive. It retrains."

Megan nodded slowly.

"The labyrinth isn't punishing us. It's teaching us. Each room is a lesson. Each stranger is a lesson. The building isn't a monster. It's more like a curriculum. It's a correction."

"And it stops teaching when we've learned the lesson," Megan said, her tone somewhere between a question and a statement.

"Yes."

"That's why the hallways are shortening."

"Exactly."

• • •

While Frank and Megan were at the map, Dave and Pat were with Walter.

A little after eight that morning, Dave Fernandes opened the door and Pat Monteiro followed him in. The door closed behind them. The room was just as it had been the night before: one armchair, a brass-pull lamp, and Walter sitting with his hands on his thighs, his VFW cap on the small table to his left. Over the last twelve hours, Dave had realized that the cap was probably the most important thing in the room. A man kept his cap close.

Walter did not look up when they came in.

Dave carried a folding chair under his arm. He had brought it from the fellowship hall since there was only one armchair in the room. He had decided during the night that he wouldn't stand over a man who was sitting. He placed the chair two feet from the wall to Walter's left and sat down. He didn't face Walter directly, but sat a little off to the side, the way he used to sit next to his own father at a counter.

Pat hadn't brought anything. He stood in the middle of the room with his hands in his khaki pockets, shifting his weight from one foot to the other.

"Walter," Pat said. "Listen. We've been trying to figure out what the building is. Anything you can tell us, like when you got here, what you've seen, or if you've met anyone else, would help us. We have a theory that..."

Walter did not raise his eyes.

Pat managed to say another sentence and a half before he realized how he sounded. He stopped and looked at Dave, but Dave did not look back. Dave kept his eyes on the light.

Pat stood still for another long minute, then walked to the wall across from Dave and sat down on the floor with his back against the plaster. As he lowered himself, his knees made the familiar sound they had for fifteen years. He stretched his legs out in front of him and stayed quiet.

All three sat in silence.

The room was quiet, but not like the fellowship hall. The fellowship hall's quiet felt like everyone was holding their breath. This room's quiet had settled in over years, the kind that comes when a man no longer expects anyone to break it. Sitting in his chair, Dave realized that silence was what made Walter feel at home. Silence was where Walter belonged.

After about ten minutes, Dave reached into his jacket pocket and pulled out a pack of Wrigley's spearmint gum. He usually kept it in his truck's glove box for long drives. On Wednesday, he brought it from the cab because his mouth was dry, and since then, he had chewed a piece every hour for thirty-six hours.

He held the pack out to Walter without looking at him. He offered it at arm's length, the way someone might hand a tool to a coworker.

Walter looked at the pack. Then he reached out, slowly, and took a stick. He did not unwrap it. He laid it across the arm of the chair beside him.

Dave put the pack back in his pocket.

• • •

Time passed in the room without anyone noticing.

Pat was the one who finally broke the silence. He hadn't meant to. He did it the way he did most things, by trying to fix what was in front of him.

"Walter," he said. "My father served. Vietnam. Twenty-fifth Infantry. Came home in '69 and never said a word about any of it. I asked him once, when I was seventeen, what it had been like, and he looked at me and said, Patrick, there are things you don't put in a son's head. That was the only sentence I got out of him. He died in 2003. I sat with him at the end and I did not ask him again. I have spent twenty-some years wishing I had."

He stared at the floor as he spoke.

"I'm telling you that because I think the reason I didn't come find you, when you came to that Christmas Eve service two years ago and sat in the back, is that I have spent forty years not knowing how to talk to a man with that kind of cap on. I would rather walk past him than say the wrong thing. And I am sorry. I should have said the wrong thing. The wrong thing would have been better than the nothing I gave you."

Walter did not move.

They sat in silence for a long time.

At last, Walter asked, "What was your father's name?"

Pat looked up. "Tony. Tony Monteiro. Out of Provincetown."

"Tony." Walter repeated the name, as if weighing it. "I knew Tony overseas. He was a kid from Provincetown, just eighteen."

Walter stopped. His hands, which had been flat on his thighs, closed slightly.

"Tony pulled me off a trail in '68 thirty seconds before the trail went up. I was new. He had been there six months. He saw something in the dirt I didn't see and he put a hand on my chest and walked me back ten paces, and the man who came up behind us where I had been standing did not get walked back, and that man went home in pieces, and I went home whole. I never thanked Tony for it. I told myself I would, when we got out. We got out and I didn't. I went to Lowell and Tony went to the Cape and the years went the way the years go."

He paused.

"In '04 I read his obituary in the Cape paper. I drove down to Provincetown for the wake. I sat in the parking lot for forty minutes. I could not make myself go in. I drove home. That is the closest I ever got to saying thank you to your father."

The room grew quiet.

Walter stayed silent for a long time. He didn't cry or look at either of them. What he had said had taken something out of him, and it showed only in his now closed hands.

Dave stayed still. Pat stayed quiet.

After a while, Walter picked up the stick of gum from the arm of the chair. His hands shook a little as he unwrapped it and put it in his mouth. He folded the foil wrapper and tucked it into his shirt pocket, as if saving a receipt.

He chewed slowly.

He did not say anything else for a long time. Dave and Pat were silent too. The three of them remained where they were, and the silence changed. It was no longer the quiet of someone alone, but the quiet of three men who had silently agreed to stay.

• • •

As Frank and Megan studied the map, the building kept getting smaller.

Ray returned from his third visit to Darnell and said that the back emergency exit, which had led to the impossible staircase on Wednesday night, now opened onto the parking lot, just as it was supposed to. He didn't go outside. He paused in the doorway, felt the October wind on his face, then turned back inside. He planned to stay with Darnell until Darnell asked him to leave.

Dave Fernandes and Pat Monteiro were still with Walter. The door stayed closed. They hadn't come out.

The Youngs led Sarah out of her room and back into the original sanctuary, which they could reach again. Sarah trembled. Linda walked beside her. They helped Sarah to the back pew, the same one she had sat in alone eight months before. Ellen sat on her left, and Linda sat on her right.

By now, there were only about eight people left in the fellowship hall. The others had either left or gone further inside.

The building was now only a small part of what it once was.

• • •

Frank looked at Megan across the map. He still had one last question.

"Megan."

"Yeah."

"The labyrinth hasn't given you a stranger. Every other adult has been matched, even the ones who barely talked at the potluck. Everyone has a door. You don't."

"I was going to ask you about it too but I think I know why."

Frank waited.

"It tried. I think it tried the first night. When I went into the labyrinth with you on Wednesday and Thursday, I kept feeling like the hallways were pushing me somewhere. But when I got there, nobody was there. I think it tried to match me, and then it stopped trying."

"Why would it stop?"

"I think...I think it was because I was already with people before the building started to change. I just didn't realize it counted."

Frank held her gaze.

Megan continued. Her voice was steady, the same way it sounded when she worked at the sound board.

"I've been coming to this church alone for three years. My parents are divorced, and neither of them cares about any of this. I don't have a ride home on Sundays, so I drive myself. I sit at the sound booth and run the morning. I know the people here. I know Joanne's kids' names. I know which pew the Cabrals sit in and which one the Medeiros kids use. I bring Betty Sullivan coffee with one sugar when she's here. I'm not saying I'm a saint. Trust me, I have more crap than most in my life. I'm saying I was already here, Frank. I think I was just doing it from the sound booth."

She paused but Megan was not done. Frank waited.

"When I was twelve, the year my parents split, I started coming here on Sunday mornings because the house was quiet in a wrong way and the church was quiet in a different way. Nobody asked me why I was here. Grace gave me a Bible the second week. Tom showed me the sound booth the third month because he saw me watching the levels from the back and figured I was bored. I wasn't bored. I was paying attention. Nobody else was paying attention to anyone in particular, so I started paying attention to everyone. I learned the names because nobody was going to learn mine."

She realized what she had just said and stopped.

"That came out bitter. I guess it is…It is bitter. That's the part I've been hiding."

She put the pencil down.

"I've been keeping a ledger on this congregation for two years, Pastor. Not on paper, just in my head. I notice who doesn't say hello to Sarah. I notice who walks past Betty's pew without making eye contact. I notice who used to come to the welcome table and stopped after their husband stopped coming. I tell myself I'm noticing because someone should. But I'm also noticing because nobody noticed me, and I wanted, in some small mean part of me, to be the one keeping score. Don't get me wrong. I love these people. I do. But the spite was real too. Both feelings have been with me at the sound booth for two years."

She took a deep breath.

"I think the building tried to give me a room because of the ledger. That's what the rooms are for, right? For the things you can't see in yourself. And I think it stopped trying because, sometime in the last fourteen hours at this table, I started crossing names off it. Not all of them. Not even most. I'm not done being angry. But I crossed off enough that the hallways stopped nudging me anywhere, and I don't think I want to be the one keeping score anymore. I think I want to be the person who knows the names without also keeping a list of who owes her."

She looked up at him.

"That's the closest I can get to saying it."

Frank looked at her and felt like he was looking into a mirror. He had spent hours slowly admitting the same kind of thing she had just revealed in only two. He never realized she was carrying it. He did not even know she was carrying anything at all.

"I didn't know."

"Nobody knew. That's the thing. Nobody writes any of this down."

She picked the pencil back up. She didn't meet his eyes for the next minute, the way teenagers do after saying the truest thing they've ever said out loud and pretending it didn't cost them anything.

• • •

Frank looked at the map, then at the pine door Megan had marked with a small letter F. The stone in his jacket pocket felt hot. It was the hottest it had ever been.

Frank stood up.

Megan did not stand. She stayed at the map.

"I'll be here."

"I know."

"Frank?"

"Yeah."

"Whatever's behind that door. It's yours. Nobody can go with you."

"I know."

• • •

Frank left the fellowship hall through the connector door and entered the labyrinth.

The hallway stretched out in front of him, just as it had for every parishioner who had gone to their door. He kept his hand in his pocket on the stone and walked.

The pine door waited at the far end of a quarter-mile corridor, and Frank walked toward it.

Part Three

The Strangers

Chapter 10

Frank Alone

The connector door closed behind him. The fellowship hall fell away.

Frank didn't rush. He walked slowly, a pace that felt unfamiliar. For twenty years, he had moved through this building from one job to the next. Now, he wasn't just between tasks. He was heading somewhere, and this time, the destination was his choice.

He looked back through the connector door before it closed. Megan stood at the map table. She looked up and gave him a single nod.

He knew that would be the last bit of reassurance he'd get from anyone for a while. He was grateful Megan hadn't made it into something bigger.

His phone buzzed in his pocket.

He pulled out his phone. He had two bars of service, more than he'd had in forty hours. There was a text from Janet.

Just heard. Are you all right?

He stared at the message. He began to type, stopped, then tried again.

I'm fine. There's something I have to do here. I'll be home tonight if I can.

He almost sent it. The words were the same ones he'd used for twenty years: pastoral, reassuring, and just vague enough to ease Janet's worry without inviting more questions. He read the message before sending it and realized what it really was.

He erased it.

He typed instead: *I am in the building. I am safe right now. I do not know when I will be out. There is something I should have done a long time ago. I will tell you everything when I get home.*

He hit send before he could revise it.

He stopped in the hallway, phone in hand. After twenty-eight years of marriage, he realized he might never have sent Janet a message admitting he'd failed at something in his work as a pastor. Janet had carried the weight of his ministry without ever being recognized. She made the meals, answered the phone when he was at the hospital, and dealt with late nights, missed dinners, and parishioners who saw her only as Frank's wife. She never complained. Until now, he had always taken her silence to mean everything was fine.

His phone buzzed once. *Okay. I'll wait.* He read those three words and understood right away that Janet had been waiting much longer than the last forty hours. She had been waiting for years.

He put the phone back.

He kept walking.

• • •

At first, the corridor looked just like the building he knew. Fluorescent tubes glowed in the mid-century fixtures Megan had once dated. Pine baseboards matched the 1924 original. The paint was a shade lighter than in the fellowship hall, the way paint always seems to lighten when the same formula is used decades apart.

He passed a framed photograph of the 1978 expansion crew. Seven men in overalls, one of them a young Ray, next to a cement mixer.

He had walked past this photo twice a day for twenty years.

But now the photograph hung in a hallway the church had never had.

He kept going.

The trim grew thicker. The baseboards became wider. The fluorescent tubes were replaced by pendant fixtures on chains, dark brass, a style he guessed was from around 1890. The floorboards beneath him were wider and darker now—pine, hand-planed and oiled, with an authenticity you couldn't fake.

He walked past a framed print on the wall. It was a hand-tinted page from a nineteenth-century religious periodical. He didn't recognize it, and he knew no one from the church had put it there.

The corridor grew narrower.

The ceiling dropped by a foot. The woodwork reminded him of what he'd seen in restored houses in Plymouth and Duxbury, the kind made before factory milling. The walls were plaster and lath. A draft came from somewhere he couldn't find. There was nothing outside these walls to cause it, but the draft was there anyway.

The corridor narrowed once more.

He had to turn his shoulders a bit so his jacket wouldn't brush the wall. The floorboards were uneven now—wide, hand-hewn pine, laid on sleepers that had settled into the earth long ago. A small leaded window sat high in the west wall, though he knew the real church didn't have a window there. The light through the panes was the wrong color for an October afternoon on Cape Cod. It looked like the kind of light afternoons had before cities and glass factories.

He paused under the window and looked up. The glass was bubbled, so old that the air inside had never been breathed by anyone from his century. Beyond the window wasn't Cape Cod. Beyond the window wasn't anything at all. Whatever sun shone through those panes had set three hundred years ago.

He kept walking.

The corridor didn't open up, but it changed.

Plaster walls gave way to bare timber. The floorboards were so wide they must have come from trees that no longer grew in New England. The ceiling was uneven, as if the person who cut the beams hadn't bothered with a level.

At the end of the corridor, maybe two hundred paces away, stood a door. It was pine, aged to the color of old leather, with an iron latch instead of a knob.

Frank didn't flinch at any of it. He had spent his whole adult life preparing to walk through American religious history. He just had never walked through the part that was his own.

• • •

The walls along the last stretch were covered with photographs. These weren't paintings or engravings, but photographs in modern frames. Frank stopped at the first one and looked at it. Even before he finished taking it in, he realized he had seen it before.

It was a new-members dinner in October 2019. Eight people sat around a long table in the fellowship hall. Frank was at the head, smiling with a paper plate in front of him. He remembered the dinner and thought it had gone well.

He looked at the eight people and counted them. None were members anymore. Seeing their faces, he realized he had known each for about three months but hadn't spoken to any in three years. One woman, whose name he thought was Patricia, came to mind. He wasn't sure that was right. He hadn't thought of her since her son's baptism in 2020. He didn't know she had moved to Florida or that her husband had died last spring. Grace had told him during coffee hour in May. Frank had said that's so sad and meant it at the time, but he hadn't done anything with the news. He hadn't called, sent a card, or visited her son's house in Falmouth, just four miles from the church.

He wondered how he could be unaware of these things. But deep down, he knew. He had a habit of pushing them out of his mind. He called it the demands of the calling. It sounded respectable, and it had worked for him for twenty years.

He kept walking.

There was a mission trip to Guatemala in the summer of 2021. Tom organized it, and fourteen people from the church went. Frank flew in for three days midweek because that was all the time he could spare.

One photograph showed Frank at an orphanage, holding a small child and smiling for the camera.

He remembered taking that photo and posting it on the church's Facebook page. When he returned, he preached a Sunday sermon about going to the nations.

He couldn't remember the child's name—he hadn't learned it. He was there for three days and took nine photos. In his sermon, he hadn't mentioned a single Guatemalan by name.

He moved on.

There were Christmas pageants—ten years of them. Each year, Frank wore a different sweater and guided children in bathrobes through the Nativity story. The same forty families came year after year. Frank smiled in every photo, but he couldn't name most of the children.

There were potluck photos too—Wednesday after Wednesday. Ray sat at the head of a table, Grace brought her Corningware, and Frank moved between tables, laughing and shaking hands.

There was a picture of a potluck three weeks ago, during a youth event. Tom posted the photos himself. In one, Frank appeared in the background, walking past a group of teenagers. He recognized his own profile.

He couldn't tell from the photo which teenager was Jaylen.

He looked at that photo for a long time before moving on.

There was a hospital photo of Betty Sullivan in a rehab bed, waving at the camera after her hip replacement. The church's card sat on her bedside table. Frank recognized it—he had signed it, but hadn't delivered it himself. He left it in Grace's mailbox with a note for Betty, since Grace visited the rehab facility twice a week and Frank only went once during her two-month recovery.

A photograph showed a child dedication. A baby in a white gown, parents on each side, and Frank holding the baby at the front of the church. Frank couldn't remember the family. He tried. The parents' faces looked familiar, like faces in a crowd. He couldn't recall their names.

Another photograph showed a funeral. The casket was closed in the sanctuary, the congregation wore dark clothes, and Frank stood at the pulpit. He remembered the funeral and the eulogy he wrote that morning in about forty minutes. He couldn't remember if he had called the widow in the months since. He was pretty sure he hadn't.

The last group of photographs was just one frame, hanging alone at eye level.

It showed the front steps of the church on a Sunday Frank couldn't place. A man was walking down the steps, balding and middle-aged, wearing a suit that didn't quite fit the occasion. Frank didn't remember the man. He couldn't tell from the photo if he had been at that service.

Below the frame, taped to the wall on a small rectangle of index card, was a caption in Megan's handwriting. visitor, did not return.

Megan had kept a binder. Frank hadn't known. Frank had not known a lot of things.

• • •

He stopped somewhere along the last stretch. The weight of the photographs was too much to carry all at once.

He took the stone out of his pocket.

He hadn't held it in his hand, outside his pocket, since Sunday afternoon, when he sat in his office and turned it over on the blotter next to the broken stapler. Now he held it in his open palm. Nothing visible — no glow, no tremble, no pulse. To anyone outside him it was an ordinary stone with a quartz vein through it, slightly darker on one face, strangely oval, just warm.

He looked at it. For the first time, he understood it completely.

The stone's warmth felt like another person's hand because what it carried was human. The people who hanged Rebecca Nurse had warm hands. They wrote their sermons with warm hands. They took communion with warm hands. They quoted Scripture in courtrooms with warm hands. It was warm the same way his own hand had been when he didn't reach out to a woman crying on a park bench.

The stone carried the warmth of hands that held God's Word but not His people. The warmth stayed in the stone because it had never cooled in three hundred years of American Christianity.

He put the stone back in his pocket.

He wasn't done carrying it. He kept walking.

• • •

He reached the end of the corridor.

The door stood before him. It had settled a bit in its frame, like old wood does, and now it hung a little crooked.

This was the last closed door in the building. Frank just knew it. The signs had started to make sense to him earlier that morning, and he realized—just as Megan had when the hallways began to shrink, and Ray had when Darnell said look at me—that the building was speaking to him in a way he couldn't ignore.

His stranger was behind this door.

He stopped at the doorway and finally allowed himself to wonder who might be waiting.

Frank knew the answer. Still, he had avoided saying the name out loud. Yesterday, Megan had said it for him in the kitchen doorway, her voice as flat as when she tested the microphones. Marcus Leite. They had talked for half an hour in Frank's office six years ago, but Frank never called him back. The name stayed with Frank, like the impression of the stone on his blotter.

Now, he allowed himself to say the name in his mind.

Marcus.

He had failed many people. Twenty years. Hundreds of parishioners. Thousands of moments. Countless small lapses in attention. He remembered Patricia. He remembered the Guatemalan child whose name he never learned. He remembered the balding man in the Sunday suit who walked away from the church. He remembered the woman on the park bench in Salem six days ago, who couldn't be behind this door because they were strangers to each other.

But Megan had named one.

Frank had an idea. He wasn't sure, and he didn't want to be sure before opening the door. If he knew, he would have to face what came next, and he wasn't ready. Even after twenty years as a pastor, he still didn't know who he had failed most. As he stood at the iron latch, he realized that was the real problem. It wasn't just having a name in his mind. The real issue was that the name had been there for six years, and he had never faced it.

The stone in his pocket was hot now. It wasn't painful, just warm, like a hand that has held yours for too long.

Frank put his hand on the latch.

He did not lift it.

His hand was on the iron. Ready? Not quite. But he was more ready than he had been on Wednesday, when he walked the first quarter-mile with Megan and turned away from the door. More ready than on Thursday, when he sat in the fellowship hall and listened to others go in. More ready than this morning, when Grace called him Pastor for the first time in a week.

He wondered if he should pray. He couldn't find the words. For twenty years, he had preached about prayer and offered hundreds of prayers from pulpits and at bedsides, but none of those words fit what he needed now.

He kept his hand on the latch in a hallway that seemed to hold him in place, focusing on whoever was behind the door. Frank didn't speak to God or ask for anything, unsure if he even had the right. He just held there, and deep inside, something like a prayer began, even though he didn't know how to begin.

He lifted the latch.

Chapter 11

Marcus

The door swung open, not in any dramatic way. The iron latch lifted, the hinges made a brief noise, and then the door finished moving. The room beyond appeared.

The room was small, maybe ten feet by ten. Its walls were bare timber, and the floor was wood. There was just one window, set high in the far wall, with the same bubbled, leaded glass as the corridor. The light coming through looked pale and old.

A folding chair stood in the middle of the room. It had a metal frame and a blue vinyl seat, just like the chairs in the fellowship hall at Cape Community Church.

A young man sat in the chair.

He had short, dark hair and wore a grey hooded sweatshirt, jeans, and new-looking sneakers. He had no coat. He sat with his forearms resting on his thighs, hands folded, eyes on the floor. When he looked up, his face was familiar—the kind of familiarity that comes from knowing someone since they were a baby.

Frank paused suddenly in the doorway.

Frank knew the name. He almost said it, but stopped himself. For the first time, he wondered if he should.

Marcus Leite was twenty-four now. Fourteen years earlier, Frank had baptized him in the portable tank they used for spring baptisms. He had also spoken at Marcus's grandmother's funeral when Marcus was twelve. Frank knew his parents, but they stopped coming to church when Marcus turned nineteen. Back then, Frank told himself they had their own reasons for leaving. Marcus's face, neither smiling nor glaring, reminded Frank of something he had seen once before, six years ago across his office desk: the look of someone who had waited a long time and wasn't sure it had been worth it.

"Hey," Marcus said.

"Marcus."

111

"Yeah. It's me."

Frank hadn't entered the room yet. He remained in the open doorway.

"Can I... can I come in?"

"Yeah. I mean, you opened the door."

Frank stepped in. The door stayed open behind him; he didn't close it. There wasn't a second chair in the room.

He looked around for a place to sit.

Frank sat down on the floor.

• • •

Neither of them spoke for a while. Frank had his hands on his thighs, palms down. The stone in his jacket pocket was hot. He was aware of it the way he was aware of his own pulse.

He let the silence linger. For years, he had always been the one to break it, but this time he chose not to.

Marcus spoke first.

"I didn't — I didn't plan what I was going to say. I thought I would, you know, on the walk here, but I don't actually remember walking here. One minute I was at a bar on Main Street in Hyannis and the next minute I was in this room. I've been in this room for, I don't know. Days. Or whatever counts as days in here." He rubbed his face with both hands. "Anyway. I didn't plan."

He looked at the floor.

"Let me just say it. I want to just get it out. Is that okay?"

"Yeah. Yeah. Of course."

"I'm not going to, like, rehearse it. So it might come out wrong."

"That's fine."

Marcus took a breath.

"I went home that night. After we talked in your office. You know what night I mean."

Frank remembered. It was six years ago, when Marcus sat across from him and admitted he wasn't sure he believed anymore. Frank told him his doubts were just a phase and that he needed to trust the Lord more. He said it kindly and firmly, with the confidence of someone who had faced the same struggle in seminary and made it through.

"I went home and I lay on my bed for four hours. I didn't sleep. I kept, like, replaying what you said. Trust the Lord more. I kept hearing it. Over and over. It was the thing my grandmother used to say. It was the thing you said at her funeral. I trusted the Lord. I trusted the Lord my whole childhood. And then I got to a point where I couldn't. I didn't know how… and I came to you, and you told me to go back to the thing I was telling you I couldn't do."

He rubbed his hands together slowly.

"You know what the worst part was? You weren't mean about it. You were nice. You were really nice. You poured me a coffee from that little machine you have in your office and you sat in your chair and you explained it to me like I was a, like I was a freshman in a theology class and I'd just asked the first question in the syllabus. And I remember thinking, sitting there, he doesn't understand what I'm saying. He thinks this is a question. It wasn't a question, Pastor. It was a drowning."

Frank's hands were flat on the floor. He was listening.

"Two weeks later I was on the floor of my bathroom at four in the morning googling how to know if you are a real Christian. Which. I mean. If you're ever up at four in the morning googling that, by the way, don't. It doesn't help."

He made a small, dry sound that wasn't quite a laugh.

"Six weeks after that I stopped being able to go into church buildings. Not just Cape Community. Any church building. I had panic attacks. My chest would tighten up and my hands would go numb and my vision would close in from the edges, and I'd have to leave. I'd sit in the parking lot in my car and wait for it to stop. That lasted about two years."

Frank struggled to keep his face calm. He realized he was listening more to facts than to the person in front of him, and that mattered. He wanted to bridge that gap, but he wasn't there yet.

He thought, I could have helped him. Then he corrected himself: No, I couldn't have. That was the point.

He remembered seeing him in the parking lot once, maybe a year after he left. He thought he saw him from his office window, then went back to his desk. But he wasn't sure if that memory was real or just something his guilt created. That uncertainty felt like its own accusation.

"I failed a semester of school. I didn't tell my parents. I transferred. I went to therapy, eventually. About a year after things got really bad. The therapist was a woman named Rebecca who'd grown up Catholic and left. She was good. She was really good."

He stopped for a second.

"The faith I have now. If I have one. And I think I do. It's not the faith you taught me. I'm not going to go into what it looks like, because I don't owe you that. But I wanted you to know it exists. It's small. It's honest. It's built on the pieces of the old one that didn't break."

He glanced over at Frank.

"That's what happened. After."

There was a long silence, maybe a full minute.

Frank finally said, "Thank you for telling me that."

"I didn't tell you that for thanks."

"I know. I'm sorry. That was the wrong thing to say."

"Yeah."

• • •

There was another silence. Frank rested his hands on the floor. He had been sitting on the cold pine boards for ten minutes, and his back was already aching. That ache felt like the most normal thing in the room, and he was grateful for it.

He started to speak.

"Marcus, I remember that conversation differently than —."

"Don't."

Frank stopped.

"Don't tell me how you remember it. Please." Marcus stared at the floor. "I've been in here thinking about how you remember it. I know what you remember. You remember a kid in your office with some theological questions. You gave him a pastoral answer, he left, and he didn't come back. You figured he'd sort it out. Maybe you thought about it for a couple of weeks. Then you moved on."

Frank began to speak...

"I'm not done."

Frank closed his mouth.

"I'm not here to yell at you. I don't even — I don't know why I'm here. Maybe part of me wants you to say you meant well. But I already know that. I know you meant well, Pastor." He paused. "That's not what hurt me. What hurt me is that meaning well isn't the same as being what someone needs. I needed you to know the difference, and you didn't."

Frank didn't answer right away. He was thinking, and his thoughts moved at two speeds. The first was professional, the theologian in him hearing an argument and sorting through its structure, testing its claims against what he knew. The second was slower, and it was the one that mattered. That was when Frank realized this wasn't an argument. It was a report of pain.

Frank tried a different angle. His voice was lower.

"I was trying to reassure you. I thought — I had been there. I had doubts myself in seminary, and I worked through them, so I thought —"

"That's exactly it."

"What?"

"That. That right there. You thought. You were doing thinking. I didn't need your thinking. I didn't need your reasoning. I needed you to say you didn't have the answers either."

Frank stopped.

He listened to what Marcus had just said. He had heard similar things before—at conferences, from younger pastors who had struggled, even from Janet once or twice in their twenty-eight years of marriage. But until now, he had never thought it applied to him.

"I —"

He did not finish.

Marcus spoke in a low voice, almost a whisper. "Take your time."

The room was so quiet it felt like time had stopped. There was no hum from the lights, no ticking from the baseboards, and no sound from the hallway. The labyrinth was silent, as if the room had finally found its purpose.

Thirty seconds. Frank stared at the floor between his knees.

"I was doing the best I could with what I had."

He whispered it. He believed it. He realized he had been holding onto that defense for his entire ministry without knowing it.

Marcus let Frank's words hang for a moment.

"Frank. I don't think that's true."

"No, I — Marcus, I —"

"It's not that you weren't doing your best. It's that your best wasn't what you were supposed to do."

Frank went still.

"Your best was giving a theological answer to a kid who was asking for help. You had the job. You had the training. You had twenty years of reading, seminary, and pulpits. And you had something I needed, but I'm not sure what to call it. Company. Presence. Whatever Grace has." He paused. "That part of the job, you weren't doing. I don't think you had done it for anyone for a long time before you met me."

Frank had started to cry.

He had not done this in front of a parishioner in thirty years of ministry. He was not sure his body could still do it. His eyes filled with tears, but he did not sob, and he did not wipe them. Wiping them would mean moving, and he did not trust himself to move.

"Marcus."

"Yeah."

"You're right."

Frank looked down at the worn floor.

"About which part?"

"All of it."

· · ·

Marcus had stayed steady through most of the conversation. Now his voice grew thick. He finally spoke about what he had carried for six years.

He looked at the floor and spoke.

"I didn't stop believing in God." He paused. "I stopped believing in you."

The words lingered in the air. Frank felt them deep in his chest.

Marcus kept going because he had started and needed to finish.

"I want you to understand what that was like. Because you didn't. I don't think you realize that, for a teenager, it's the same thing. You were God's representative to me. When I was six, you were the voice of God. When I was thirteen and my grandmother died, you told me she was with Jesus. When I was seventeen and confused about what I believed, you were the one I turned to. At eighteen, I didn't have a way to separate my pastor from the church. There was no line in my mind. I wasn't old enough to make one."

Frank had his hands flat on the floor on either side of him. He was looking at Marcus without moving.

"So when I walked out of your office that day. And you did not call me. And you did not come to my house. And you did not check in with me at any point over the next three years while I was falling apart." He swallowed. "When that happened, Frank, I did not lose faith in some bad pastor. I lost faith in the entire system that you represented to me. You were the church. You not caring was the church not caring. And it took me two years with

Rebecca to separate the two of you in my head. And I am still, at twenty-four, working on whether I actually believe any of it."

He paused and rubbed his eyes with his hand. When he lowered it, his eyes were wet, but his voice stayed steady.

Frank stayed quiet. He was determined to let Marcus finish, no matter how long it took.

"I came back. Not to church, but to faith. I don't go to Cape Community. I'm not going back there. Now I go to a small church in Centerville that meets in a community center. I sit in the back, and sometimes I cry. The pastor used to be a cop before he was ordained. He knows who I am, and he doesn't try to fix me. That's what I have now. That's what I think God rebuilt. Without you. Despite you."

He caught himself.

"That came out harder than I meant. I don't mean it as a dig. I'm telling you what happened. That's all I'm doing."

Frank kept looking at him. Tears ran down his face, and he no longer tried to hide them.

Marcus spoke in a near whisper.

"I'm not mad at you anymore. I stopped being mad about two years ago. I just wanted you to know. I just wanted you to know what it was."

• • •

When Frank finally spoke, he stumbled over his words.

"I want to say. I'm so sorry that —"

He stopped. That was not it.

Something changed in the room before Frank could figure out what it was. The temperature dropped sharply, like it does in a walk-in cooler when the compressor turns on. He could see his breath, and the hair on his arms stood up. He looked at Marcus, who was watching him, and saw Marcus's breath too. Deep down, Frank realized the room had been listening, and it didn't like what it heard.

"Marcus, what I want to say is, I didn't know what it looked like from your side. I didn't..."

No. He caught himself doing it again—trying to explain, to put the truth inside something bigger so he wouldn't have to feel it as it was.

The walls groaned.

It was the real sound of wood under strain—the kind you hear on a ship in rough water or a barn in a winter storm. But Frank wasn't in a ship or a barn. He was in a small Puritan room that had been a church on Cape Cod just hours before, and the walls groaned as if something was pushing from outside. He glanced at the wall behind Marcus, unsure if it had moved. When he looked back at Marcus, the far wall seemed closer than before. Maybe his eyes were playing tricks on him. He couldn't tell.

He stopped.

He closed his eyes for a moment.

The room didn't wait. Frank felt it through his hands on the floor—a slow pressure, as if the space was shrinking. The floorboards didn't move, but it felt like they might. The leaded window high on the wall was farther from the ceiling than before, either because the ceiling had dropped, the window had shifted, or both.

"I keep trying to say the right thing, but I keep getting it wrong. Let me just say what's true."

Marcus waited. He didn't help Frank, and he wasn't going to. That wasn't his job.

Frank spoke again, this time more slowly.

"I was wrong."

The room held.

It did not expand. It simply stopped contracting, like holding your breath at its highest point, waiting to see what would happen next. The groaning faded. The cold stayed, watchful, but did not get worse. The two of them sat in a small room that now felt even smaller. Frank realized the room was listening, and for once, he did not try to qualify what he said.

"I was wrong that day in my office. I have been wrong every day since. I was wrong to tell you your doubts were a phase. I was wrong to frame my answer as a reassurance when what you needed was somebody to be in the mess with you. I was wrong not to call you. I was wrong not to come to your house. I was wrong not to notice when you disappeared from the congregation. I was wrong to tell myself your parents left for their own reasons."

He paused.

"They left because of what I did to you. I was wrong about that too."

He was aware, saying this, that the inventory was not complete. It could not be complete. Twenty years of pastoral ministry was twenty years of

Marcuses he had not known about. Twenty years of people who had come to his office and left with the answer he had instead of the answer they needed. Marcus was the one the building had shown him but Marcus was not the only one.

The words came out in clumps, like stones from a pocket he had filled over the years. As he spoke, the cold faded. There was no warmth yet, only the loss of its sharp edge. His breath was no longer visible. He had not noticed when it disappeared.

"And I am not going to pretend I know how to make it right. I don't. I don't think you're asking me to. I don't think it is something I can make right. I think what I did cost you years of your life you cannot get back. And I have to carry that. And I don't know yet what carrying it looks like or what it means."

He looked up at Marcus.

"I don't know how to fix it, Marcus. I don't know if it's fixable. I don't know what to do with the fact that you were a kid who needed me, and I gave you a lecture instead of what you needed."

He kept going.

"I don't know. But I see you. I am looking at you and I am seeing a man I helped break. And I know I helped break him. I know I hurt you. And I am not going to stop seeing that now. I see you."

Marcus looked at him for a long time.

Neither of them spoke.

"Okay," Marcus breathed. Only the one word.

It was not I forgive you, and it was not it's okay. It was just the only word Marcus had for what Frank had said, the only word he could offer.

The room exhaled.

The walls that had felt so close now seemed to move back. The ceiling rose, and the far wall behind Marcus shifted to where it should have been when Frank first entered. The leaded window sat higher, and the pale old light coming through it looked warmer on Marcus's face. The cold left the room the way it leaves a kitchen when the oven is left on. It didn't make a sound. It was just gone.

A long silence followed. Both men sat on the floor. At some point during Frank's apology, Marcus had moved down from the folding chair, though Frank hadn't noticed when. They sat against opposite walls with their legs stretched out, and Frank realized the walls were farther apart than before. The folding chair sat empty between them. The silence stretched on. The building stayed quiet.

After a while, Frank said, "Can I ask you one thing?"

"Yeah."

"Why did you come tonight? You said you didn't know how you got here, and I believe you. But if you had known—if the building had given you a choice—would you have come?"

Marcus thought for a moment. He rubbed the back of his neck and looked up at the leaded window.

"I'm not sure. I think so. I guess I've needed to say that for a long time."

Frank nodded.

"Can I ask you something?" Marcus asked quietly.

"Anything."

"Are you going to do this differently? After?" He paused. "I don't mean with me. I mean in general. Are you going to be different?"

Frank took his time before answering. He wanted to say yes, but he knew he couldn't promise Marcus anything. The only promise that mattered was the one he kept, and the only way to keep it was to begin tomorrow.

"I hope so. I don't know. I'm going to try."

"That's all I was going to ask."

Neither of them moved for a while. The room stayed quiet. The labyrinth was silent. The stone in Frank's jacket pocket felt hot, and still, neither of them moved. Frank couldn't hear it, but he felt the building shift deep in his bones.

It wasn't dramatic. Just a settling, like the way a house relaxes in cold weather.

The labyrinth had heard them.

Chapter 12

Dead Rock

Frank and Marcus stayed on opposite sides of the room. They hadn't said much since Marcus agreed. The silence felt different now. Before, it was heavy with unfinished business. Now, it was just two men who had said what they needed to, sitting together in the quiet that followed.

The corridor outside the door was shorter now. Frank could see it from his seat. The Puritan-era hallway he had walked for what felt like a quarter-mile was down to about forty feet. The bare timber walls were smoothing out as he watched. It wasn't happening quickly, more like how ice melts in a warm room. The floorboards grew narrower. Plaster covered the timber, then smoothed into beige paint. The building seemed to be shedding its layers, one by one, returning to the original church with its shell parking lot and the view of the sound.

He watched a leaded window in the far wall simplify into a pane of ordinary glass and then close over entirely, the wall sealing around it the way a wound heals in time-lapse. He watched a doorframe from the colonial stretch of corridor lose its wide trim, the profile thinning from handworked to machine-milled, century by century, until it matched the trim in the fellowship hall. The photographs that had lined the Puritan corridor were gone. The walls were clean.

The building was not being exorcised. It was simply shrinking. The spirit, or whatever it was, had not been forced out. It had just been starved.

Frank got up slowly. His knees hurt and his back felt stiff. At fifty-two, after sitting on a hard bench for two hours, his body made it clear why he was sore.

Marcus stood up as well.

They looked at each other.

"Is it over?" Marcus asked.

"I think so. I think the building is going back."

Marcus looked at the corridor. The Puritan walls were gone. Now, it just looked like a hallway.

"Going back to what?"

"To what it was."

"Was it always this?"

Frank thought about the question. He looked at the hallway, now maybe thirty feet long and still getting shorter.

"Yeah," he said. "I think it was always this."

• • •

They stepped into the corridor. It was about twenty feet long now and getting shorter. At the far end was a door that hadn't been visible an hour ago. Or maybe it had always been there and was just visible again—the fellowship hall connector.

They walked toward it. Frank kept his hand in his pocket, holding the stone. It felt cooler than it had in the room with Marcus. Not cold, just cooler. He noticed but said nothing.

The connector door opened from the other side.

Megan was standing in the fellowship hall doorway. She held her phone in one hand and a rolled-up bulletin-map in the other. The map was useless now, and she knew it. She held it like a technician holding a tool after finishing a job.

She looked at Frank, then at Marcus. She didn't ask what had happened. She had spent twelve hours with the map, which had told her everything, hallway by hallway, in paces and timestamps.

"The building is going back," she said.

"Yeah."

"The exits started opening about four hours ago. Grace went out first, then the Bentos, the Monteiros, Joanne and the boys. Most of the congregation is outside."

"Tom?"

"He's still with Jaylen. Jaylen's room opened into the sanctuary about twenty minutes ago. They're in there now. Tom has his feet up on a pew."

Megan looked at Marcus again. She didn't know him. She studied him the way she would study equipment she hadn't been briefed on.

She reached out her hand.

"I'm Megan."

"Marcus."

She turned and walked back into the fellowship hall. Frank and Marcus followed her.

The fellowship hall looked the same as always. The food tables were still there, cleaned and wiped down. The coffee urn was turned off. Folding chairs lined the walls. Only Megan's map table remained, covered with bulletins full of notes about a place that no longer existed. Frank paused at the table and studied the map. There were handwritten notes, colored dots, steps, and timestamps. It was a seventeen-year-old's full account of something supernatural, written in ballpoint on the back of a church bulletin. He placed his hand on the paper, just as Ray had done two nights before.

They walked from the fellowship hall into the foyer. Everything was as it had been. The bulletin board still held its announcements. The missions envelopes sat in their wooden box. The guest book lay open on the table, untouched for months. The carpet hadn't changed. Three jackets hung on the coat rack by the door, left there since Wednesday night. One belonged to Marjorie.

The hallway from the foyer to the sanctuary was thirty-two feet long. Frank didn't measure it. He didn't have to.

He walked the hallway, all thirty-two feet. Each step felt right. The framed photo of the 1978 expansion crew hung in its usual spot. The bathroom door with the dripping faucet was where it always was. The supply closet where Ray kept the tape measure was at the far end. Nothing was out of place or changed.

Frank and Marcus walked side by side, but not close together. They stayed silent. What lay ahead was the rest of their lives, and the quiet filled the gap between what had been said and what would be lived.

Megan walked ahead. Her phone stayed in her back pocket. She didn't take any photos. Now, the building was just a building.

They passed Frank's office with the door open. Frank glanced inside as he walked by. He saw the desk, the broken stapler, and the blotter with a small oval mark where the stone had rested from Sunday to Wednesday. The books were still sorted by tradition, with the Patristics on the south wall catching what little light there was. The window faced south, dark now, but in daylight it would show the parking lot and the sound beyond. His laptop was still open to the Edwards document, the cursor blinking where he had left it four days earlier.

He would return to that office on Monday and sit at the same desk. He would look at the sermon he had started about Jonathan Edwards and the Great Awakening, the second in his four-part series on the American church, and wonder if he could preach it as he had intended. The series was about what happens when Christianity forgets who it is for. He had planned to tell the congregation, not to show them.

He didn't yet know what he would do differently. He only knew the office would feel different because he would be different, and that change was not a transformation but a new direction.

They reached the front door.

As they walked by the sanctuary entrance, Frank glanced inside. The pine pews showed the same dark shine from years of lemon oil. The platform was simple. The upright Yamaha piano still had its sheet music from Wednesday. In the back, Megan's headphones rested on the mixing board.

Tom sat in the back pew with his feet up, still wearing the long-sleeved T-shirt he'd put on after giving Jaylen his hoodie. Jaylen lay next to him, curled up with a blanket, asleep at last. His face was still tense and pale, but at least he was resting, unlike twelve hours before. Tom's hand rested on the back of the pew close to Jaylen's head, not touching, just nearby.

Tom noticed Frank standing in the sanctuary doorway and nodded. Frank straightened up in response. They didn't say anything. Tom had been sitting there for hours and wouldn't leave until Jaylen asked him to.

• • •

Frank paused at the front door. Through the window above, he saw the first gray light of morning spreading across the Cape Cod parking lot.

He pulled the stone from his pocket. It now felt cold, just a lifeless rock. The stone seemed dead because, for two nights, the church had been alive.

Frank turned the stone in his hand and held it up to the morning light. The dark, scorched mark he'd noticed at Proctor's Ledge still seemed to be there—or maybe it was just the natural color of New England granite, like the rocks found from Gloucester to Falmouth. In the Saturday morning light, it looked like any other stone, the kind a child might skip across a pond.

He remembered Cotton Mather on horseback. He pictured Nicholas Noyes beneath the hanging bodies, calling them firebrands of hell. He thought of the Puritan corridor and the leaded window lit by a sun that had set three centuries ago. His mind wandered to the woman on the bench in Salem, and finally to Marcus, waiting just behind him.

Ray sat on the floor with Darnell Foster, each against a different wall, looking at each other. Tom stayed in the pew, gave away his hoodie, and promised to remember a name. Linda sat across a table, sharing the truth about her marriage in a single breath with a woman she'd just met. Grace was on the piano bench, then on her knees, her hands always warm. Megan stood at the map, measuring the gap between words and actions.

Marcus stood three feet behind him, having built a faith from the pieces Frank had left behind.

The gap between words and actions had grown smaller, though it hadn't disappeared. It might not close in this generation, or even the next. But for two nights, a small church on Cape Cod had lived up to its purpose, which turned out to be both harder and simpler than anyone thought. It meant sitting on a floor, waiting in a doorway, or speaking one honest sentence to someone else. Just being there was enough to weaken a spirit that had survived for three centuries on absence.

He slipped the stone back into his pocket. He wasn't finished with it yet. He didn't know what he would do with it, but he still needed to carry it. Whatever it meant, it hadn't ended with the labyrinth.

Frank opened the front door.

The October air came in.

• • •

Frank walked out the front door and stopped on the top step. The morning air touched his face. He hadn't been outside for three days. He felt the cold, the salt, and the damp on his skin. He breathed in air that wasn't from the fellowship hall, and his body relaxed without him meaning to.

He saw the crushed-shell parking lot, the split-rail fence, and Route 28A. There was pitch pine across the road and conservation land beyond it. The sky was gray and a seagull flew low across the lot, heading east toward the sound.

The world was still there.

Grace knelt on the grass. Her navy cardigan was wet with dew, and her hands rested on her thighs. Frank realized she had been there for almost a day, or maybe she had left and returned. It did not matter. She was there.

She looked up at Frank, then at Marcus. At first, she didn't recognize Marcus, but then she did, and her expression changed. It wasn't surprise, but recognition—the look of someone who had been praying for people and was now seeing one of them in person.

She stayed on her knees, closed her eyes, and moved her lips as she added two names to the list she carried.

125

Marcus stepped out behind Frank, and Megan followed him.

Several parishioners who had been released earlier sat on the curb at the edge of the parking lot. They wore blankets from the donation bin and held paper cups. Their faces showed relief mixed with something harder to describe. The Bentos were there. Paul held Marjorie's hand. Pat Monteiro stood near his car with his arms folded. He hadn't driven home. He was still there.

The church was a white clapboard building with a modest steeple on a low rise above Route 28A. It looked the same as always—the building from 1924, expanded in 1978, and re-roofed last year by Joe Michaud of Bourne. It looked ordinary, just like a small church on Cape Cod. The bell in the steeple hadn't rung since 2011. The black-iron handrail Ray installed was on the front steps. The crushed-shell drive needed grading.

Frank looked out at the building, the parking lot, and the morning.

Behind him, inside the building, the hallway was thirty-two feet.

Chapter 13

October Morning

The air was salty and cold. This was the Cape.

Frank was on the front steps. He breathed in the air. He wore the same jacket he had taken to Salem and the same shoes he had driven north in. On the outside, nothing about him had changed. Inside, everything had.

The crushed-shell parking lot was half-full. Some cars had been there since Wednesday evening, dew-covered and waiting. Ray's truck. Tom's Jeep. The Youngs' Civic. Megan's moped was still by the handrail. A few sedans Frank didn't recognize had arrived overnight. They were parked at the edges as if their drivers weren't sure whether to knock on the door of a closed church before sunrise. Someone had called someone else. The outside world was just starting to notice that a few people were missing.

Frank still relied on the math Megan had taught him, so he knew this was right on time. Inside the building, he felt exhausted, as if he had been there for days. Outside, the cell tower said it was Thursday at dawn. Some spouses had stayed up all night. Others wouldn't start to worry until they had their coffee.

The strangers were in the parking lot too. They had come out during the night as the labyrinth fell apart and the building's rooms joined back with the old church. They were real, confused, and had nowhere to go.

Darnell Foster sat on the curb at the far edge of the lot, his duffel bag between his feet and his work boots laced. He looked at Route 28A, squinting as he tried to remember which way his life had been going before the building drew him in. Ray was beside him. He had been by Darnell's side for most of the last twelve hours. Ray was standing because his knees were tired of floors and curbs and anything lower than a kitchen chair, but he stayed close and wasn't leaving.

Sarah sat on the church steps, wrapped in a blanket from the donation bin. Linda sat beside her. They weren't talking. Linda's hand rested near Sarah's but didn't touch. The gap between their hands was the kind people leave when they're careful with something new. Ellen Young sat on Sarah's other side, holding a paper cup of coffee she had found somewhere.

Walter stood alone by the split-rail fence at the edge of the lot, his VFW cap on and his hands tucked into his jacket pockets. About ten feet away, Dave Fernandes leaned against the fence, careful not to look at Walter. In the past twelve hours, Dave had realized Walter didn't want direct attention. So Dave simply stayed nearby. That was what he could give.

Jaylen remained inside, sitting with Tom in the back pew.

The labyrinth had ended. The people it brought to light were still here and still needed help. Now, in the plain light of day, how the church responded—without any supernatural push—was the real test.

• • •

No one called a meeting or assigned partners. The congregation, or those who remained in the parking lot, simply started doing what the labyrinth had taught them, without needing to be told.

Ray crouched beside Darnell on the curb. His knees ached, but he ignored the discomfort.

"My house is about a mile away. I have a spare room. It's simple—just a bed and a shower. I can make you breakfast."

Darnell looked at Ray.

"You don't have to decide now. I just want you to know the offer is there."

Darnell didn't answer, but he nodded. It was the kind of nod someone gives when they're offered something they're not sure about but might accept. Ray stayed crouched beside him.

Tom walked out of the sanctuary with Jaylen. Jaylen stood upright but looked unsteady. He still wore Tom's hoodie, the church logo across his chest, the zipper undone because his hands hadn't been steady enough to zip it three days earlier. Tom held his car keys.

"Cape Cod Hospital has a detox program," Tom said. "I called them from the church phone about ten minutes ago. They know we're coming."

Jaylen got into the Jeep. Tom closed the passenger door, glanced at Frank across the parking lot without waving or calling out, then got in, started the engine, and drove away. The shell crunched under the tires as the Jeep turned onto Route 28A heading east toward Hyannis, and soon it was gone.

Linda removed her jacket and draped it over Sarah's shoulders, on top of the blanket. Sarah accepted it without protest. Linda offered no explanation.

Dave reached into his jacket and pulled out a pack of gum. He offered a piece to Walter without meeting his eyes. Walter accepted. After a while, Walter said, "Thank you, son." Dave nodded but kept facing forward. In twelve hours of waiting, Dave had learned that Walter would speak when he was ready, and the best thing Dave could do was stay steady when it happened.

These were small gestures, not big endings. Ray offered a spare room, not a plan. Tom drove to the hospital, not to preach. Linda gave a jacket. Dave gave gum. These simple acts showed up for someone, and they marked the start of whatever would follow.

• • •

Marcus was by the front steps after leaving the building. He didn't join the others or talk to anyone except Megan, who nodded at him by the moped. He watched the parking lot from afar, feeling separate from what was happening.

He slipped his hands into his grey hoodie and turned toward Route 28A.

Frank noticed him.

Frank wanted to go after him. He had felt this urge for thirty years. Call out. Say something caring. Finish the moment. Marcus, wait. Let me give you my number. Can we get coffee this week? Can I check in? These thoughts came easily to Frank. He had been helping people leave for twenty years.

But he stayed silent.

He watched Marcus walk across the crushed-shell lot toward the road. Marcus never looked back. He moved like a twenty-four-year-old finally stretching his legs after being indoors for three days. He also moved like someone who had already said what mattered and wanted to go before anything could change it.

Frank watched him go.

The relationship was still broken. It would not be fixed today. It might never be fixed while Frank was alive. What happened in that room was not a healing. Marcus finally spoke about what he had been holding inside. Frank listened. The distance between them, which had been growing for six years, was now out in the open. Seeing the problem was not the same as fixing it, but you cannot fix what you cannot see. Frank let the wound remain a wound.

He had never done this before. He was used to managing goodbyes. He would always suggest a follow-up, offer a call, or plan the next step. He liked to close the loop, because leaving things open felt like failure to him. In a way, it was about control. By shaping how someone left, he could stay in charge of a story that was never really his.

Marcus reached Route 28A and turned right toward Mashpee. Frank did not know if Marcus had a car, or what had brought him from a bar three days ago to that room. He did not know if Marcus would return to the church in Centerville or read the Bible again. Frank did not know what would happen next, and for the first time in his ministry, not knowing did not feel like a failure. It felt like respect.

He watched Marcus walk until he was just a small figure on the side of the road. Frank kept watching a little longer, until Marcus turned a corner and disappeared.

Grace, on the grass, opened her eyes. She had been watching too. She looked at Frank, and he looked back at her. They stayed silent. Grace gave him a single nod—the same nod she had given him for forty years. The nod that meant yes and I see and that was right.

• • •

The parking lot eased into an ordinary morning. What had been extraordinary was fading, not all at once, but slowly, as each normal detail returned.

A Falmouth police cruiser drove slowly up Route 28A, maybe checking on the church. It kept going.

Janet arrived around nine and parked beside Frank's Camry, which hadn't moved since Wednesday night. She got out and walked to the front steps, taking her time. She didn't ask what had happened. She placed her hand on Frank's arm, and he covered it with his own. They stood together quietly.

Frank had been married to Janet for twenty-eight years, but he couldn't remember ever holding her hand in public on the church steps. He had always managed their image and the routines of Sundays, but never just stood with her and held her hand. Now he did. He felt her shoulder against his arm and noticed again how perfect she was, something he hadn't thought about in years because he'd stopped seeing her as a person and more as part of his routine. She was a person—the one who had stayed with him through every failure shown in the corridor photos. She hadn't left him, and now she was here on an October morning that felt like three days to him, but for her, it was just one phone call and a worried drive down Route 28A.

Tonight, he planned to tell her what had happened in the building. He would talk about Marcus and about the woman on the park bench he hadn't stopped for. He would share things she probably already sensed, since Janet had been watching him for twenty-eight years and she understood. It wouldn't surprise her, but saying it out loud for the first time would still matter.

Frank's phone buzzed. He checked and saw a voicemail from Helen Bettencourt at the Mashpee Baptist food pantry. He didn't need to listen. He would call her back today and agree to the monthly volunteer slot, the fourth Saturday, for two to four hours.

The October light grew stronger as the morning went on. The gray sky was clearing. On a clear day, you could see Martha's Vineyard from the front steps. Today wasn't clear, but the horizon was brighter than it had been all week.

Frank and Janet were on the steps together, Grace kneeling on the grass below. The building behind them looked plain and white. The cell tower said it was Thursday, just after nine. By Sunday, in three days, he would need to know what to say from the pulpit.

Chapter 14

Titus

The church looked just as it always had. The white clapboard walls, the pine floors darkened by years of lemon oil, the familiar pews, and the modest platform were all unchanged. The upright Yamaha piano stood uncovered this morning, waiting for Linda, who had not yet arrived.

The parking lot was only half full. Frank noticed this from his office window when he arrived at eight. There were eleven cars instead of the usual twenty. Some people just hadn't returned. The building felt too unfamiliar, and the confrontation had been too personal. The Monteiros, the Youngs, and Dave Fernandes were all absent. Several parishioners who had attended the Wednesday potluck were missing and likely wouldn't return next Sunday either.

Frank wasn't surprised by any of this.

Frank sat in his office with the door open. The desk hadn't changed. The broken stapler still sat beside the pen cup. The blotter showed a small oval mark where the stone had rested from Sunday to Wednesday. Now, the stone was back on the blotter, right next to that mark, just where Frank had put it this morning after taking it from his jacket pocket. It sat there, gray, cold, and still, its quartz vein catching the office light like any piece of New England granite.

A dead rock on a desk next to a broken stapler.

Beside the stone lay a single sheet of paper. It wasn't a manuscript or twelve double-spaced pages in Times New Roman tucked into a black leather folder. It was just one page, handwritten in Frank's neat, tight script. There were only a few sentences, some crossed out and rewritten. It was the shortest sermon Frank had ever prepared, and the first he had written by hand since seminary.

This time, he didn't rehearse. He didn't read through the opening or check the timing. He skipped all his usual routines.

He picked up the sheet, folded it, and slipped it into his jacket pocket. When he stood up from the desk, the stone stayed behind, visible through the open office door to anyone passing by in the hallway.

He walked down the hallway to the sanctuary. It was thirty-two feet away.

•••

Frank came into the sanctuary through the side door. He stayed away from the platform. Standing at the edge of the room, he looked around to see who was there.

Grace sat in her usual spot: second pew on the right, wearing her navy cardigan and holding her leather Bible with the tabs. She had always been the first to arrive for forty years, and she was first again today.

Ray sat in the third row, but not in his usual seat. He had moved over one spot because someone else was next to him. Darnell Foster sat beside Ray, wearing a clean button-down shirt that was obviously Ray's, though it hung loose on his shoulders. Darnell kept his hands in his lap and studied the bulletin he'd received at the door, reading it slowly, as if he was relearning a language he used to know.

Sarah sat in the back row with Linda beside her. They had arrived together. Linda hadn't played the piano yet this morning. She sat with Sarah now, and when she went up to play, she would return to this seat afterward.

Tom sat in the fourth row, not checking his phone because he had left it in the car. He wore a plain grey T-shirt since his hoodie was at Cape Cod Hospital with a seventeen-year-old he had promised to remember. The seat next to him was empty, and he had left it that way on purpose.

Megan manned the sound booth with headphones around her neck, the board levels set and the call-to-worship slide ready. She had arrived before Frank.

Joanne was here with her boys. Eli sat up straight, which was something new for him.

Marjorie Bento came without Paul, who had stayed home. She hadn't said why. Frank guessed Paul still didn't know how to handle what had happened in the building, but Marjorie came anyway. She hadn't missed a Sunday in forty years and wasn't about to start now. Frank hoped Paul would come next week, though he didn't count on it.

Janet sat in the second row on the left. Frank couldn't remember her ever sitting there before. She usually stayed in the back, where pastors' wives sat so they could greet people as they left. Today, she was up front, watching Frank with the steady look of someone who knew her husband was about to do something difficult and wouldn't look away.

There were about thirty people here, though two weeks ago the room would have held sixty.

Frank looked at everyone, noticing where they sat and how the room felt different. The change was like a sermon before the sermon: these people had chosen new places.

• • •

The service began as usual. The call-to-worship slide appeared on the screen. Linda played the opening hymn on the piano. The congregation stood and sang. Their voices were softer this time, since there were fewer people, but the small group felt genuine and sincere.

Frank led the pastoral prayer without using an index card. He prayed from where he stood. The prayer was brief and included names that had never been in a pastoral prayer at Cape Community Church.

He prayed for Jaylen, who was at Cape Cod Hospital this morning.

He prayed for Darnell, who was in the third row.

He prayed for Sarah, who was in the back.

He prayed for Walter, whose last name he still did not know...for now.

He prayed for Marcus.

He spoke Marcus's name from the platform, even though most people in the room did not know who Marcus was. He offered no explanation. He simply said the name.

He also prayed for those who were absent. He did not mention any names. Frank simply said, "Lord, be with the ones who could not come back. We understand why."

Grace said amen.

Megan adjusted the microphone slightly because Frank's voice was quieter than usual. As always, she was paying close attention.

Frank walked to the pulpit and took out a folded sheet of paper. He unfolded it, placed it on the pulpit, and smoothed it with his hand.

He looked up.

• • •

He opened the Bible on the pulpit to Titus. He read aloud.

"They profess to know God, but they deny him by their works. They are detestable, disobedient, unfit for any good work."

He let the words hang in the silence. Earlier this week, the same verse had been read in this building at two in the morning by a woman who did not need a pulpit.

He turned to Titus 3. He read verses 3 through 8:

For we ourselves were once foolish, disobedient, led astray, slaves to various passions and pleasures, passing our days in malice and envy, hated by others and hating one another. But when the goodness and loving kindness of God our Savior appeared, he saved us, not because of works done by us in righteousness, but according to his own mercy, by the washing of regeneration and renewal of the Holy Spirit, whom he poured out on us richly through Jesus Christ our Savior, so that being justified by his grace we might become heirs according to the hope of eternal life. The saying is trustworthy, and I want you to insist on these things, so that those who have believed in God may be careful to devote themselves to good works.

He set the Bible down. He looked at the paper. He looked at the congregation.

"For years I taught you what those verses meant. I was — I was good at it. I could break down Titus for you. I could explain the Greek, the historical context—Paul writing to a young pastor on Crete, trying to build a church where people didn't want one. I gave you all of that. You sat here and listened, and I was proud of that work."

He paused and glanced at the paper.

"I did not live it."

He let the sentence linger the way he had with the verse. Then he went on.

"I'm standing here telling you that I didn't live these verses. Not the first, not the last, not any of them. I spoke from this pulpit every Sunday for twenty years. I used good theology, good grammar, and most of the time, real conviction. I believed every word I said up here. I still do."

"But in my actions...in my actions, I denied Him. In the way I lived out what I believed…in being present for the people God put in front of me, I denied Him. I chose studying over visiting. I chose the sermon over the person. I chose being right instead of just being there."

He paused and looked out at Grace.

"That's the same sin Nicholas Noyes committed under the hanging tree in Salem in 1692. I'm not saying this to be dramatic. I say it because the Bible says it. It's the same sin, just in a softer form and with better manners, three hundred years later. Noyes quoted Scripture at people he was killing. I've quoted Scripture at people I was overlooking. I'm not sure which is worse, but I know they're the same thing."

His voice grew quieter.

"And some of you paid the price for that. Some people aren't here today because of what it cost."

The sanctuary was silent. No one was waiting for the next point in a sermon.

"I'm not going to explain what happened in this building this week. Some of you were here, so you know. Some of you weren't, and I don't think I could explain it in a way that would make sense. But I can tell you what I learned."

He looked up from the paper. He didn't need it for this part.

"I learned that grace teaches. That's what Titus 2 is about. The grace of God has appeared, and it teaches us. It doesn't just save us, it teaches us. And what it teaches—what it taught me this week in this building—is that the work of the church isn't just the sermon or the theology. It's the person right in front of you. The one you haven't bothered to ask about. The one you drove right past."

He stopped, then began again.

"…The person you walked by when you knew they needed you."

He folded the paper and slipped it into his pocket.

"I don't know how to do this differently yet. I'm not sure I know how. But I want to try. And I want to start with you."

He didn't say amen. He stepped down from the platform, sat in the chair behind the pulpit, and rested his hands on his knees.

• • •

No one clapped. No one said amen. No one came up to Frank afterward to tell him it was one of his best.

Through the open office door at the end of the hallway, the stone sat on Frank's desk. Gray and cold, it was just a dead rock beside a broken stapler on a blotter. The oval impression would fade over time, the way all impressions do.

Linda stood up from the back row and walked to the piano. She sat at the bench, paused for a moment, looked at the keys, and placed her hands on them.

Grace picked up a hymnal from the rack in front of her, turned to a page, and held the book open.

Linda began to play, and the congregation stood.

The singing was soft. Half the voices from two weeks ago were gone. But those who remained were present in a new way, and the sound was not just people performing a hymn. It was people singing because, this morning, the words were true. They had started to live them, not just believe them.

At last, they were singing for the people in the back pew, the ones who had come once and were never asked their name.

Chapter 15

Epilogue

Six Months Later

April

The fellowship hall smelled of coffee, donated pastries, and the special warmth that comes when a room is used for its true purpose.

It was Wednesday, just after noon. The potluck tables remained, but three days a week they were covered with paper tablecloths and set with coffee urns, sandwich platters, and sometimes a box of muffins from the Dunkin' on Route 28. The muffins were always from the day before and always gone by one. The bulletin board now had a hand-lettered sign reading COMMUNITY DROP-IN, listing hours for Tuesday, Wednesday, and Thursday, 10 to 2. Ray had added a note in his handwriting: Coffee is free. So is the company.

Ray stood behind the table in a flannel shirt with rolled-up sleeves, pouring coffee from a twelve-cup Mr. Coffee he bought last November. He said the old forty-cup percolator was a relic from a time when they made coffee for themselves. Now, the percolator sat in storage, and Ray did not miss it.

The room was not crowded. Six or eight people sat around, which was typical for a Wednesday. Two were regulars Frank knew—men from the neighborhood who started coming in December and kept coming because the coffee was good and Ray never asked them to sign in. Another was a woman Frank did not know, sitting alone with her cup and her phone, avoiding eye contact. Frank did not know her story, and he did not need to yet. She was here, and that was enough for today.

Darnell was not there this Wednesday. He had been coming and going since October. For two months, he stayed at Ray's house, sleeping in the spare room Ray offered him one morning in a parking lot and eating dinners Ray's wife cooked without complaint. In January, Darnell found a room through a program in Hyannis. He still came to the drop-in center most Tuesdays. He and Ray played cribbage with the same deck of cards Paul Bento used to keep in his jacket pocket.

The drop-in center wasn't a program. There were no intake forms, no mission statement, and no funding except what Ray took from the general fund with the deacons' approval, plus the casseroles Grace brought without being asked. It was just a room with coffee, sandwiches, and a man who showed up three days a week because, back in October, he learned what it meant to show up. It was messy, imperfect, and real. Frank, watching from the hallway, thought it was the first thing the church had done in twenty years that Titus would have recognized. The verse said to be careful to maintain good works. Good works, not good theology or good sermons. Good works. The verse never said they had to be elegant.

• • •

Frank sat in his office with the door open. The hallway stretched out for thirty-two feet.

The desk hadn't changed. The blotter was the same too, though the oval mark where the stone used to sit had faded to almost nothing—a faint shadow you'd only notice if you knew to look. The stapler was new. Frank bought it in January after the old one jammed for the last time on a bulletin insert. He'd kept the broken one for three years. It only took him five minutes to replace it at Staples. He wasn't sure why he waited so long.

The stone sat on the desk, where it had been since October. It looked gray, cold, and ordinary, with the quartz vein still showing. Over six months, it had just become a paperweight. Sometimes Frank put papers under it, but most days he didn't think about it. It was just a rock on a desk.

The church had gotten smaller. On a good Sunday, thirty-five people showed up. Some who left after the labyrinth never came back and probably wouldn't. The Monteiros moved to Florida in January. Dave Fernandes joined a church in Mashpee that was closer to home. The Youngs were still gone. Frank prayed for them by name every Sunday.

The ones who stayed really stayed. Grace sat in her usual spot, second row on the right, every Sunday, her Bible filling up with more tabs. Ray stopped counting the offering behind closed doors and started doing it at the drop-in table where everyone could see. Linda still played the piano with her eyes closed, but now she sat in the back row before and after the service, next to Sarah, who had filed for divorce from the deacon in Orleans and was living in a room Linda found for her in Falmouth. Tom still ran the youth group, but he stopped calling it that and started calling it Tuesday nights, since not all the kids were from the church and some weren't even kids.

Megan was eighteen now and had been accepted into the engineering program at UMass Dartmouth. She would leave in September. She'd already trained her replacement at the sound booth, a fourteen-year-old named Chloe who was eager but a little slow on the slides. Megan didn't seem worried about the change. She told Frank, in her usual flat voice, that Chloe would figure it out. "She pays attention," Megan said. "That's the main thing."

Frank wanted to tell Megan what she meant to the church, but he didn't. He was starting to realize that what he most wanted to say was often what the other person didn't need. He'd write her a short letter in September. Somehow Frank would make sure Megan knew.

Janet started working part-time at the Falmouth library in January. She didn't ask Frank what he thought. She just told him at dinner, as casually as if she were mentioning a dentist appointment. He said that's great and meant it, never thinking about whether her hours would clash with church events. Sometimes they did. If a co-worker called out, she missed Wednesday potluck, and Frank made his own dinner. The first time he stood at the stove with a pan and a half-frozen chicken, he realized he hadn't cooked for himself in twenty-eight years. He ate at the kitchen table with a book open beside his plate. The book was Bonhoeffer's *Life Together*, which he hadn't read since seminary.

• • •

His phone buzzed on the desk beside the stone.

A text came in from a number he didn't recognize.

I'm reading Titus. It's not what I expected.

Frank picked up his phone and read the message. He stared at it for a long time.

The number wasn't saved in his contacts, but he didn't need it to be. He knew who it was, just like he had known six months ago who was behind the door when he stood at the iron latch.

He read the message again: I'm reading Titus. It's not what I expected. Twelve words—the most Marcus had said to him in six months. Frank stared at them and felt his old habit return, the one that had shaped his ministry for twenty years: answer right away, say something meaningful, show you're the pastor with all the answers. He could already feel his reply forming. That's wonderful, Marcus. I'm so glad. Titus is one of my favorites.

The grace passage in chapter two is where it really opens up. Can I suggest a commentary?

He did not send that.

He put the phone down on the desk beside the stone. He looked at the two objects side by side on the blotter: the phone with Marcus's twelve words on the screen, and the stone that had started it all. Both, in their own way, seemed to be waiting for Frank to decide what to do next.

Frank would reply, but not with a sermon, a reading list, or an invitation that tried to guide someone else's faith. He would keep it short, leaving the conversation open for Marcus.

He didn't know yet what he would say. Maybe he'd figure it out tonight, or tomorrow. He would let the reply come at Marcus's pace, not his own.

He picked up the stone instead.

. . .

He slipped the stone into his jacket pocket. This jacket was lighter than the one he wore to Salem last October. The stone settled inside, cold and small.

He left his office and walked down the thirty-two-foot hallway. He passed the fellowship hall, where Ray washed mugs and a woman he didn't know sat with her coffee. In the foyer, the guest book lay open to a page with three new signatures this week. He stepped outside and down the steps into an April afternoon on Cape Cod.

The air felt different than in October—warmer, but still sharp. It was the kind of spring New England offered slowly, with salty air and a wind that still remembered winter. The pitch pine across Route 28A looked greener than it had six months ago. The sky seemed higher. On clear days, you could see Martha's Vineyard from the front steps, and today, there it was, a dark line on the horizon.

Frank got into his Camry. It was the same car, with the same Gordon College sticker on the rear bumper he'd never removed. He drove south toward the water. The drive took about two minutes.

He parked at the town beach. The lot was empty, as it usually was in the off-season, the kind of parking Cape locals enjoyed between Labor Day and Memorial Day. He walked across the sand to the water's edge.

Vineyard Sound in April was grey-green, cold, and restless. The tide was partway in. The sand at the water's edge was dark and packed, scattered with small stones and shell fragments the ocean left behind and reclaimed, the ordinary geology of a coastline shaped long before anyone was there to see it.

Frank took the stone from his pocket and held it in his palm, turning it over once. He noticed the quartz vein, the grey color, and its ordinary weight. He had picked it up behind a Walgreens in Salem six months ago, as he often did at historical sites, not knowing then what he was really picking up.

He didn't throw the stone into the ocean. That would have been a gesture, and Frank was finished with gestures.

He crouched and placed the stone at the tideline, in the wet sand, where the water might take it or leave it. The next wave reached it and flowed around it without moving it. The following wave touched its edge. The stone stayed in the sand, dark, wet, and unremarkable.

Frank stood up and watched the stone for a moment. Then he turned and walked back to his car.

He needed to visit someone in the hospital—a church member he'd meant to see for three weeks. He had put it off, as he often did, but today he was finally going. That was what mattered now. Not the stone, the labyrinth, or the sermon he would give on Sunday about what grace had taught him and was still teaching him, one visit, one name, one person at a time. The real work was in the doing. He hadn't realized this until a building showed him, a seventeen-year-old mapped it, and a seventy-year-old woman knelt in the grass and prayed for the names he should have been praying for all along.

He got into the car and started the engine.

The stone was never the problem. It had only ever been a mirror. For the first time in his ministry, Frank was moving toward what it had revealed to him.

Faith by itself,

if it does not have works,

is dead.

James 2:17

If you enjoyed this book? Please consider taking just a few seconds to leave an honest review on Amazon. Reader reviews mean everything to authors, and your input helps new readers find their next book. Even if you leave just a "star" review it will help a lot. Thank you so much!

Appendix

Historians generally agree on twenty executions and several prison deaths from harsh conditions, illness, neglect, or inability to pay jail fees after acquittal during the hysteria. Sources vary slightly on the exact number of prison deaths, commonly four to six named adults, with some noting up to thirteen possible additional casualties and occasional mention of an unnamed infant. The list below includes all documented named accused individuals who died during the period.

May 10, 1692

Sarah Osborne — Died in prison (Boston jail; due to harsh conditions and illness). She was one of the first three accused.

June 10, 1692

Bridget Bishop — Executed by hanging. The first person executed in the trials, at Gallows Hill / Proctor's Ledge.

June 16, 1692

Roger Toothaker — Died in prison (Boston jail; conditions and possible mistreatment).

July 19, 1692

Five executed by hanging at Gallows Hill

Sarah Good. Rebecca Nurse. Elizabeth Howe (sometimes spelled How). Susannah Martin. Sarah Wildes.

(Note: Sarah Good's infant daughter, Mercy Good, also died in prison sometime before this date due to the conditions, though she is not always named separately in victim counts.)

August 19, 1692

Five executed by hanging at Gallows Hill

George Burroughs. Martha Carrier. George Jacobs Sr. John Proctor. John Willard.

September 19, 1692

Giles Corey — Pressed to death, with heavy stones placed on his chest in a field near the jail. The only use of this torture method in colonial New England. He refused to enter a plea.

September 22, 1692

Eight executed by hanging at Gallows Hill, the final executions

Martha Corey. Mary Eastey (or Easty). Alice Parker. Ann Pudeator. Wilmot Redd (or Wilmott Redd). Margaret Scott. Samuel Wardwell Sr. Mary Parker.

Additional documented prison deaths

Accused individuals who died in custody after the main execution period.

September 26, 1692

Rebecca Addington Chamberlain. Died in prison.

October 27, 1692

John Durrant. Died in prison.

December 3, 1692

Ann Foster. Died in prison. She had been convicted and sentenced to hang but died before execution.

March 10, 1693

Lydia Dustin. Died in prison. Acquitted of witchcraft charges but unable to pay jail fees and remained in custody.

These events are all drawn from primary court records and contemporary accounts.

About Ye Author

The Author at Proctor's Ledge

Phillip Andrade has spent more than forty years in ministry—long enough to have shepherded teenagers, served as a missionary in Japan, and survived two long-term senior pastorates in New England with both his sanity and his sense of humor still mostly intact. Raised in Falmouth on Cape Cod, Phillip has spent the vast majority of his life in Massachusetts, with the notable exception of those years spent serving in Japan. His journey of faith took a definitive turn at the age of 18 when he trusted in Jesus just before entering college—a decision that would set the course for the rest of his life.

Along the way, he picked up a B.A. in Archaeology, an M.Div. in Theology, and a D.Min. in Leadership Development, confirming that he is both formally educated and unusually skilled at remaining awake during very long lectures.

His lifelong fascination with history tends to leak into everything he writes. Ancient ruins, colonial New England, and the global upheaval of World War II all hold a particular grip on his imagination. If there is a crumbling stone wall, a weathered document, or a half-forgotten story, he is probably already wondering what happened there—and who did not tell the whole truth about it.

At heart, Phillip is a pastor who believes the Scriptures are meant not only to be understood, but lived—daily, visibly, and measurably. He has spent decades urging the local church to move beyond "what does the Bible mean?"

toward "what does it actually call me to do?" That conviction finds its way, one way or another, into everything he writes—even, as it turns out, fiction.

To support his pastoral habit over the years, he has moonlighted as a police officer, graphic designer, and firearms instructor—which means he can preach a sermon, design the bulletin, and arrest you for not reading it carefully. He also dabbles in bladesmithing because the only thing better than crafting sermons is crafting objects that, in a previous century, could demand one.

This novel marks his first venture into fiction—an unfamiliar but intriguing departure from his usual world of Bible studies, sermons, and overly technical theology papers. While he is more at home parsing Greek verbs than plotting suspense, he has discovered that stories, like sermons, have a way of uncovering truth—sometimes more sharply than expected.

He and his wife have been married for over forty years, have four children, and enjoy a plethora of grandchildren—a biblical term meaning more than you can conveniently count, especially at Christmas.

Now adding novelist to a long and slightly unpredictable résumé, Phillip brings together history, faith, curiosity, and just enough mischief to keep things interesting.

You can follow him, if you dare, at www.phillipandrade.com

ADDITIONAL BOOKS BY THE AUTHOR

- **In Other Words - Unlocking Biblical Greek: A Beginners Guide to the 10 Core Greek Words from the New Testament.** Word Studies For Small Group and Personal Spiritual Growth

- **Restored to Lead:** A Self-Leadership Manual to Break Free from Burnout and Renew Your Purpose

- **What Your Pastor Wishes You Knew:** Spiritual Drifts That Grieve the Heart of a Shepherd

- **Laura the Leaf and the Great Fall:** A Story of Staying Rooted in Love and Strength (Children's Book)